A Cruel Moon

Olivia Enclosure

Contents

Chapter 1

L iam holds me down to the floor while I punch him in the neck. He loosens his hold which allows me to jump on top and kick him in the stomach.

"Say that I win!" I demand "Alright Rylee you win. Just get off of me" he says while coughing from the lack of air.

I jump off of Liam with a lot of excitement that I was able to win a fight with him. Our werewolves are the most competitive with each other so this feels great.

Eventually I help Liam up because he is still a good friend of mine. "Don't get used to that. I'm going to win next time""Rematch tomorrow?""Absolutely. Do you want to grab some dinner""Sorry I can't. Have to check up on Scarlett""Can I join?", he asks playfully. I know Lucas and about everyone else in this pack has a crush on Scarlett. She is blessed with beautiful strawberry blonde hair and blue eyes. Plus she is a extremely nice and innocent which also makes her a target.

"Only if you get the Alpha's permission" I say jokingly why running to the Alpha's house. I see Scarlett reading a book on the couch which is typically. I see today is another book studying about mate bond.

"Scarlett, are you still dreaming about your mate", I tease her. She is 18 years old now, 4 years younger than me, and already talking about how all she wants is to meet her mate.

"Rylee! I missed you" she comes up to give me a hug.

"Sorry I was training with Liam""Oh I wish I could train with you and Liam!", she wines which is typical for her. I do feel bad with how many restrictions she has. "Come on, lets go get dinner with the pack".

The alpha let's me take her to the pack house to mingle with others as long as I promise to watch her every step. I know there are many threats against her so I understand his rules.

Liam's joins us at the dinner table and we start talking about random stuff like usual. Scarlett gives me a little kick under the table when he comes by. I may have told her I thought he was sexy and now she thinks we have something going on. If only she knew, he and all the young males were all attracted to her.

With my auburn hair and brown eyes, I barley stand out next to her. However, I am very proud of my warrior status and how much training I have been through which I know she always dreams of.

While we continue to mingle with all the pack members, the warning sirens go off. I immediately go into warrior mode and grab onto Scarlett to protect. I see Alpha Sam running into the pack house sending out orders to the top ranks. He then comes up to us as Scarlett runs up to him to give him a hug.

"Rylee you know the plan. Protect my daughter" I nod my head and drag Scarlett out of the house. I have been studying all the plans Alpha Sam has created for his daughter. He even create back up plans for all possible scenarios that could happen.

I grab Scarlett and run out of the house. I then start sprinting to the southeast side of the forest. "Rylee where are we going? This isn't the safe house" "Scarlett listen carefully. You need to do exactly what I say. This is what your dad planned for you. There is a real threat after you and my life is on the line if the plan goes wrong."

Thankfully Scarlett nods her head and follows me through the forest. When we get about two thirds in I see the marked tree with the crescent moon.

"Liam?" I whisper out. He has always been assigned as my partner for these missions so I know is he trustworthy.

"Rylee" , he whispers back and then comes in front of me to give me a hug. "Do you think this is a real threat?", he asks me. "Yes I do. I saw Alpha's face before I left. He was very serious. We can't fail" , I whisper to him very quietly so Scarlett can't hear. I know she is easily frightened.

All three of us continue to travel through the forest. Our mission is to get to Silver Heart Pack. Alpha Sam formed an alliance with Alpha Zac to protect his daughter. The only details I know about the threat is that it involves Alpha Jax from the Blood Shadow Pack. Part of my training is learning everything about every pack. I learned that knowledge is power. We know their strengths and weaknesses.

Alpha Jax is an very aggressive and ruthless. He has never found his mate but he always speaks of needing a strong alpha line to keep his pack strong. While Alpha Zac is a very thoughtful leader who also hasn't found his mate. He uses logic and respect to lead his pack which is similar to Alpha Sam.

Liam continues to lead us through another forest pass our pick boundaries. I estimate at this pace we can get to Silver Heart by the morning. Liam stops in his tracks and turns to me. I grab Scarlett's hand as a precaution and give her a hand motion to stay silent.

I hear footsteps coming from our right side. Liam transforms into his wolf and attack's the first wolf that approaches us. I motion to Scarlett to clim a nearby tree and stay on the lowest hanging branch. I see another wolf approach us so I grab my silver knife from my shoe and stab it. I found a liking to fighting with silver weapons because it allows me to stay in human form.

See Liam going after a 2nd wolf that appears, I see a man walk up to us. I sense he is a beta.

"Where's the girl?", he asks. I don't respond. I've also learned staying silent irritates your opponent which could turn into a weakness for them.

I grab my other knife from the inside of my jacket ready to attack but then I feel a hard object hit my head. My body falls to the floor but I manage to look back and see Liam also lying on the floor helplessly. I also see Scarlett still sitting on the branch staring at me.

I tab my hand on the floor twice and make sure she sees me. She nods her head in understanding. When I would train lightly with Scarlett I always taught her tapping twice is a sign of giving up. In this case I needed her to go with them peacefully and make sure they drag us with them too so we can still stay close.

Since they are ruthless it is better if she goes willingly so she is able to observe her surroundings. I give her a small smile to reassure her our fight is not over while I let the darkness take over and crash to the ground.

Chapter 2

I feel the blood running down my head from the attack. I try to move but my hands are pulled back from the silver chains on tied to the wall. Glad that trained my body to not be weakened by silver, I use all my strength to break free.

I start walking to an exit to complete the mission but then I feel my wolf stirring up from excitement which distracts me. Out of nowhere, this man appears in front of me and holds me again the wall. When I touch his skin I feel warmth and comfort and sparks. He's my mate! I look up to see my mate is Alpha Jax, the evil man that kidnapped Scarlett. I try my hardest to squirm of out his hold praying this is not real.

He laughs evilly and lifts my head to look right into my eyes, "I am going to kill you, mate."

"I reject you as my mate", I spit back in his face still trying to fight him off.

He laughs evilly, "I gladly accept you rejection. You see, I have already found my ideal mate suited for an alpha", knowing he is speaking about Scarlett.

I look up at him with clear sadness on my face. I see him looking back at me with a distracted look. I use that split second to lift my knee and hit him hard in the dick. He grunts lowly and loosens his grip on me. I take this chance to push him off and run down the hallway. I feel my wolf weakening from the rejection so I pull out all my silver knives to use as my defense.

I am able to stab a man I see guarding the door just as he was about to attack me. I hear Alpha Jax's footsteps coming near me so I open the door and continue to run out. I step outside to find that I was kept in a small cabin in the middle of the forest which makes sense since it would have taken one day to travel to the pack house.

Just as I start to search for Scarlett, I feel someone grab me from behind and carry me farther away from the cabin. Before I could scream I can sense it is Liam who is carrying me since we have always worked so closely together. The more our wolves bond, the better we can sense each other.

Once we are deep into the forest, Liam places me down which is when Scarlett runs into my arms shaking in fear.

"I will explain later, we just have to keep moving"

I nod my head in agreement, thankful Liam was able to rescue Scarlett. We run in our human form for another hour to avoid leaving our wolf scents and paw prints throughout the forest.

Liam continues to guide us since he is the most skilled with direction. He leads us to a main highway road. I sense that on the other way of the highway belongs to the Silver Heart Pack. Alpha Sam told us they are expecting us but to always be cautious of entering someone else's land. Before Liam continues further I grab his arm to stop him.

"Explain what happened" Liam shakes his head in agreement and goes to sit against a tree. I guide Scarlett to do the same with me since we all feel the exhaustion from the travel.

"They had us both tied up agains the wall with silver chains. Once they saw I woke up they called Alpha Jax to start interrogating me. But when he walked in he just stared at you and starting shaking. It was really strange but he ordered all his pack members to not touch us until he returns. The guards looked confused after he left so I took advantage of that and broke free from the chains. I saw a door near us so I just had to attack one person and then sneak into the door which lead into a hallway. I was able to sense Scarlett in another room which was only guarded by one person so I attack him and then got her out of there. I was just going back to get you at the same time you were able to escape too"

I nod my head in understanding. I know the reason Alpha Jax acted strange was because he knew I was his mate but I was too ashamed to say it out loud. My heart was still hurting from the rejection.

"Scarlett what happened to you?" I ask her. "Well after they attacked you I came down from the tree and told them I will go with them. They just kept me in the bedroom of that cabin. I didn't even talk to Alpha Jax".

I nod my head again knowing their strategy was to keep her alone and scared while they planned to get more information from us.

After a few more minutes of resting, I convince Liam it's time to meet this new pack while reassuring Scarlett that we will all be safe.

We get to the other side of the highway and slowly make our way through the forest. We try to make enough noise so we get approach soon instead of getting attacked. A few minutes later we see two wolves approaching us so we stop to show respect. The wolves transform into their human form leaving the men naked.

Scarlett lets out a gasp and covers her eyes. I try to hold back a laugh over how innocent sh is. Once they each put on shorts I elbow Scarlett so she puts her hand down.

Liam begins to speak, "We need to speak to your alpha. We are under protection of Alpha Sam".

Thankfully the warriors nod their head meaning they were expecting us and then lead us further into the forecast until we see the large pack house. We are lead inside the house which is filled with other werewolves that give us curious stares. We quickly move into the main office and told to wait for the alpha here.

A few minutes later Scarlett sits up straight and grabs my hand out of fear.

"What's wrong" I question here while Liam also looks at her confused.

The next moment we here the door open so I stand up and grab Scarlett to show respect. Alpha Zac walks in and looks directly at Scarlett then growls "Mate".

Surprisingly, Scarlett runs behind me which seems to anger Alpha Zac. I try to give him a reassuring smile. I then turn around to face Scarlett.

"Is he your mate?" She nods yes. "Why are you hiding from him?" She whispers, "He looks like he wants to eat me" I let out a small laugh at how scared she looks from her mate. "He's an alpha. That just means he likes you"

I turn around to Alpha Zac who is trying to control his wolf from getting to Scarlett.

"I'm sorry. She is just a little frightened. Alpha Sam sent us here to provide protection for his daughter which turns out is your mate".

I grab Scarlett back to stand next to me and continue to hold her hand to comfort her.

"Scarlett, just say hi" I whisper to her.

She stays in place but does wave to Alpha Zac and offers a small smile.

"Um hello I'm Scarlett"

Alpha Zac walks a little closer to her and offers his hand to shake hers. She returns the gesture and makes a some yelp noise when she feels the sparks from touching his skin.

Alpha Zac stays calm around her and doesn't try to further touch her which is a smart move. He offers us to follow him into the kitchen to get something to eat. Liam starts going through the past events with Alpha Jax and the attack while I stay close to Scarlett.

"So we think Alpha Jax is after Scarlett because of her strong alpha blood-line" Liam shares to Alpha Zac. This causes Alpha Zac to growl and move to Scarlett. Before he pounces on her I step in front of her to try to calm him down.

"Maybe just try hold her hand" I whisper to him. He nods his head and goes to grab Scarlett hand and rubs her skin. She seems hesitant at first but then holds his hand back which is a good sign.

I know I have more information about Alpha Jax but I don't want to share it in front of Scarlett. She doesn't need to know the man that is obsessed with white with her is also my mate who rejected me about 12 hours ago.

"Scarlett are you tired? Maybe you should get some sleep" "You can sleep in my room" Alpha Zac offers but she quickly shakes her head no "Maybe Scarlett and I can share a room nearby yours" I offer my option. Zac agreed and offers to show us to the room right next door to him. I let Scarlett get ready for bed first and tell her I'm going to talk to Liam before coming to bed.

I walk back down to the kitchen to find Zac and Liam discuss strategy.

"How is she" Zac asks right away. "She will be fine. Her dad just protected her from almost everything so she has to get used to being around another alpha."

"Rylee can you share how you escaped from the cabin. I realized I never heard your story yet" Liam asks.

This is what I was trying to avoid but I know it's crucial information.

"I found out Alpha Jax is my mate and then we rejected each other right after he declared to kill me in order to be with Scarlett" I say quickly while Liam and Zac let's out a low growl.

Chapter 3

After telling Liam and Zac every detail of my encounter with my ex-mate Jax, I quickly went to bed not wanting to relive the heart break anymore. Zac said he is expecting his Beta back in a few days which is when we can start discussing strategy for the upcoming war.

In the mean time Liam and I have have started to train with the Silver Heart pack warriors. I have done my training in human form only because I know my wolf is weakened.

Alpha Zac has been trying to spend most of his time with Scarlett but I warned him to take it slow so he doesn't scare her away. I usually get a breakdown of their encounters from Scarlett at the end of the day.

"Scarlett you have been reading and talking about mates for as long as I know you. Why are you so shy now that you've met yours", I ask Scarlett while we are getting ready in our room for the night.

"Honestly, I didn't think I was going to be matched with an alpha. I'm nervous from how strict and possessive they can be. I don't want to be locked up again like my father did to me"

"Listen having a mate is different. Trust me you have more control this time. Especially with Alpha Zac who is already in love with you"

Scarlett blushes from my comment and agrees to be more open with him. I bit my lip getting nervous from what I have been meaning to ask her.

"So I've been talking to some pack members around her and this one girl was having a hard time with her mate. I want to give her some advice. What have you read about mates rejecting each other"

"I did read this sad book about rejecting mates. If your mate rejects you and you accept your rejection it takes a toll on your wolf. There hasn't been a lot of studies so can't be too sure what the damage is. But good news is that there is a possibly of second change mates"

"What do you mean?"

"Well if your mate rejects you or passes away, the moon goddess has been known to create second mates as another opportunity to have a soul mate"

"But it doesn't happen for everyone, right?"

Scarlett nods her head so I end the conversation soon so she doesn't get suspicious.

After Scarlett goes to sleep, I sneak out of the house to run in my wolf form. I have been too afraid to do it in from of the pack since I don't know the damage of the rejection yet. I run through the forest to find a small pond where I transfer back in human form and put on an oversized shirt that I was carrying.

I sit near the pond letting out a cry that is long overdue. I cry for Scarlett being taken away under my watch. I cry for the moon goddess making my mate a deranged alpha who already declared his mission to kill me. After sobbing for a few minutes I clean myself up and determine to stay strong. I am a badass female warrior and will stay to protect Scarlett.

I start walking back through the forest taking my time to clear my head. I stop in my track when my wolf starts to stir inside me. I hear footsteps from behind and go into an attack stance.

A second later I see a man approaching me. From my training I know he is Alpha Zac's beta, Nathan. My wolf keeps acting excited and then I figure out why when Nathan comes clear in my view. I feel my heart stop and my breath quicken. I don't want to admit it because I can't believe it would happen so soon.

I remember from our warrior studies that Nathan's first mate died two years ago in a battle. He has been harsh ever since while Zac has stayed calm to balance the pack. I bit my lip and lean against a tree to keep from collapsing as Nathan walks closer to me.

He has an angry look on his face that is giving me horrible flashbacks from the way Alpha Jax looked at me.

He steps toward me and learns forward and runs his finger down my arm. I feel the sparks from his skin which makes this more real.

"I can't do this" he speaks. I continue to bit my lip to control my shaking.

"I can't do this again" he whispers to himself. I look down on the floor already knowing what's going to happen. The few rumors I have heard about second chance mates is that they take more work to last because the two souls have already been damaged.

A few moments pass by but I can't get myself to say anything. I feel my body go numb.

"I reject you as my second mate", Nathan speaks after a long silence. I look up into his eyes not believing that this is happening again. Surprisingly I feel more angry than sadness.

"I don't accept it" I spit out.

Nathan gets angry and throws his arms on the tree to towers over me which does frighten me a bit.

"Listen mate, you will have to accept it eventually. Do not tell anyone about this. I guarantee I will not change my mind" he threatens me and then walks towards the pack house. Once he is far enough away I fall on the ground and let out more tears.

I let myself be weak for a couple more hours before managing to walk back to the house. I am determine to get Nathan to talk to me again. I know he is scared since he already went through the loss of one mate. He wants to continue being angry at the world. What sadness me the most is that he doesn't even care what I have been through or what I want.

But I didn't accept his rejection yet. I raise my head with confidence as I sneak back to the room and shower before Scarlett wakes up. I feel determined to get Nathan to accept me as his mate.

Alpha Zac stops by to walk Scarlett and I to his office in the main pack house. I noticed they were holding hands which made me smile. At least one of us was enjoying finding their mate.

We walk into the office and my heart stops when I see Nathan inside. Alpha Zac starts to introduce us to him and my heart breaks again when he asks like he has never met me before. I follow along not wanting to anger him.

Alpha Zac begins to speak about the updates from Alpha Jax. My stomach drops from hearing his name and I try not to get nauseous.

"Scarlett's father Sam and Alpha Adrian from the Crimson Pack are coming here this week to prepare for a war. We have heard Jax is preparing his pack to attack. We believe he knows that Scarlett is being kept here"

Alpha Zac casually looks at me knowing he is keeping my secret. Even though Jax rejected me, his wolf would still be able to sense my wolf as first mates so he would be able to find me if he wanted to.

I bravely look up to see Nathan staring at me suspiciously knowing he catches the look that Zac gave me. I take his curiosity as a good sign that he is interested in me.

The next moment Liam and a few more warriors enter the office. Zac introduces then as the top male and female warriors. I notice a couple of the females stare and giggle at Nathan who doesn't return any kind of gesture. It would make sense if he is a playboy around her considering he's one of the best looking and obviously doesn't want to be committed to his own mate.

I decide to plan the next stage of my mission and befriend these women to learn more about him. I put on a fake smile and start planning training sessions with the females, Rose and Julia. I hope this works.

Chapter 4

"So who are the most eligible bachelors around here" I ask Rose and Julia during lunch the next day. They actually seem nice to talk to and it lets me have some Scarlett's has been occupied.

"Well there is Tyler who is sexy and a great dancer." Rose starts to gossip "But the big prize is Nathan. He is clearly the sexiest man in this pack plus he is a Beta" Julia adds in. "Not to mention he is so mysterious and a real challenge to get in bed with" Rose says.

"So you guys haven't slept with him?" I question.

"Not yet" Rose says with a wink"Were hoping he just needs more time since his mate passed away and then he will be willing to sleep around" Julia continues.

That gives me some hope at least. I leave lunch with a smile on my face feeling a little more confident.

Alpha Zac planned a strategy meeting now that Alpha Sam and Alpha Aiden are arriving. He wanted to get started right away on our plan since Jax could attack us any day now.

I walk into the conference room inside of the pack's prison building. I walk in to find Zac and Nathan sitting next to each other while Scarlett and her father are conversing. Liam and a few other warriors are also joining.

I sit down near Nathan who gives me an angry scowl which I try to not let that affect me. The last people to enter are Alpha Aiden and his Beta, Grayson who I recognize from my training. I recall Alpha Aiden is three years older than Alpha Zac. His pack is slightly larger as well and known for their loyalty and power.

I could feel the alpha power radiate off him as he enters. He also looks even more attractive then the pictures I studied. I feel my wolf also acknowledge his attractiveness. I hear someone clear there throat which gets me out of the trance. I see Aiden smirk at me which I then lower my head in embarrassment.

Alpha Zac starts the meeting immediately expressing how important his preparing is to protect his mate and Luna of his pack.

"Sam has told me his warriors have studying the weaknesses of every pack. Rylee can you share your findings on my pack" Zac says while staring at me.

My eyes widen that he called me out to share the flaws of his pack. I know Alphas are very proud wolves so they would not want to know what they are doing wrong. I look towards Alpha Sam and he gives me a reassuring smile.

"So from our research we found your biggest weakness is the northwest corner or your territory."

"That area is filled with steep cliffs that no one would dare to cross" Nathan interrupts me.

"Well that is not quite true. My team took a training to try to pass that area and we found a clear path that any skilled werewolf could manage".

Feeling to afraid to look at Nathan, I stare at Zac instead who looks angry.

"We didn't cross your boundary Alpha Zac. It was just to tell our theory". Alpha Zac accepts my reasoning and nods for me to continue while Nathan let's out a low growl obviously not happy with me.

"We also found that your training does not consist of any silver weapons or help to build resistance to silver while we know Alpha Jax's pack does include this in their training"

I feel Nathan getting more tense near me. I decide to look at him which is when I see the raw angry in his eyes while he looks at me. I look over to Liam right after to get him to cover for me. Since we have worked together for awhile our wolves have bonded enough to be able to sense each other.

Thankfully Liam senses my comfortableness and shares the rest of our research with the team. After much argument, specifically from Nathan, that they do not believe with fighting with weapons. They want to stay true to their wolves and use their own strength.

"Well my warriors will be using their weapons" Alpha Sam states.

"I would also be introducing weapon training with my warriors that will participate in this war. Sam, if it's alright with you, I would like your warriors to train with", Alpha Aiden also states.

I look over to him and give him a small smile which he returns. I know my wolf is weakened so my only advantage is to fight with weapons in my human form. I am glad I will still be able to train with the Crimson Pack warriors.

Alpha Zac's agrees to the plan and plans to triple training hours. Everyone agrees Scarlett is the safest with Zac so we know the war will happen here so there will be more warriors traveling here over the next few days.

As we walk out of the building, Nathan rushes out quickly so I don't get a chance to try to talk to him. I do see Alpha Adrian walking close by me so I decide to discuss the training he was interested in.

"Alpha Adrian, I would be happy to lead the training with your team with the silver weapons we were discussion"

Alpha Adrian stops walking and faces me. He is extremely tall and towers over me leaving me breathless.

"Rylee, you can call me Adrian"

When he says my name my heart stops. I just nod my head in understanding.

"Are you free tonight" he asks "For training?" "Yes. I would like to see your skills first" "Oh ya of course. I am free" "Good"

Adrian then turns around and continues walking toward the pack house. I am assuming Nathan is also in there grabbing lunch so I decide to avoid that place assuming he's still in a sour mood.

I decide to go visit the pack orphanage house instead. My parents died before I could remember anything so I was raised in an orphanage in a very small pack before I even met Alpha Sam. I try to volunteer to help the kids whenever I can.

The Silver Heart's orphanage has about twenty kids ranging from toddlers to pre-teens. Usually once you transform into your wolf for the first time you would move into the pack house to start training. I also met the two house moms that help take care of the children. Both their mates passed away in previous wars but they continue to care for the children since they were not able to have any of their own.

I spend a few hours there helping prepare lunch and then cleaning up afterwards.

I start heading back to the Alpha Zac's house since I am still staying there with Scarlett. I should ask her when she's planning to move out to Zac's room since it seems things are going well.

On my way there I see Nathan passing by. I decide to be brave and approach him.

"Hey Nathan, I was wondering if you could help improve my wolf training", I know I need him to make my wolf stronger from the mate bond.

He doesn't stop walking and bumps into my shoulder while growling out "No".

I feel my eyes water but take a deep breathe to control my tears. Instead of walking to my room, I decide to keep walking through forest to brood over my misery. I start to think if Nathan ever gives me a chance, could I forgive him for being a complete jerk to me? I know being with your mate is good for you. It completes you and makes you stronger which should what I need.

As I am walking I sense someone is near me. I stop in my tracks and pull out a knife from inside my shoe, ready to attack. The next moment I see Adrian with his hands up in defense.

"Woah Rylee it's just me" he says with a smile. That is also when I notice he is only wear a pair of shorts so he must have been on a run. I try to keep myself from drooling while I stare at his muscular abs and arms.

"Sorry about that" I respond while putting my knife down.

"Well I guess we can just start our training now" Adrian says with a smile.

"So have you played with silver before" I ask him.

Adrian walks over to me and grabs the silver knife from my hand not looking affected by it at all. He then throws it at a tree with perfect precision.

I try to hold back my blush from his impressive skills. I take another knife from my back pocket and throw it at the same tree which lands right next to his throw. He looks over at me with a smirk assuming he is also impressed by my skills.

We continue throwing the knifes for another hour giving each other tips. Adrian is surprisingly easy to talk to for being an alpha. Using they are extremely intimidating and egotistical.

I take a deep breathe and decide to ask him for a favor.

"So Adrian, do you think we could add some wolf training today?"

He looks at me curiously wondering why I would want to train in wolf form privately since that is the main form of training in this pack.

I decide to further explain. "I think my wolf is getting weaker so I have not trained with the other pack members afraid I won't be able to handle it"

"Do you know why you would be getting weaker"

"I'm I have a theory but I'm not ready to talk about it yet" trying to avoid discussing my rejection.

He continues to look at me suspiciously but finally nods in agreement. "I will help you but you have to promise to tell me your theory when you are ready"

I smile brightly at him glad to have this chance to see how much Jax and Nathan have weakened me. I agree to talk to him once I'm ready but I'm pretty sure I won't ever be ready. I'm still hoping Nathan will accept me as my mate so I won't have to worry about my wolf for too long.

Adrian starts to take off his pants in front of me which makes me yelp in surprise. Before I could cover my eyes, he has already transformed into his large grey wolf.

I take a deep breathe to try to gain some courage. I take off my clothes to transform into my average size black wolf, really hoping I don't embarrass myself.

Chapter 5

M ore warriors have started traveling to the Silver Hearts pack to prepare for the war.

Adrian and I continue our private trainings every night which I was glad he agreed to. I found that our wolves have bonded so my wolf fights really well when around him. Adrian has also been really interested in the silver knife training. It was nice being able to show your skills off to an Alpha who appreciated them.

Nathan has been avoiding me all week as well but I formulated another plan to try to get closer to him. It still hurts my wolf every night knowing he doesn't want to be with us. I've been trying to research in the library on history books of what could happen when your second mate rejects you but no luck so far.

Alpha Zac asked to meet with me so I head to his office and see him and Nathan sitting across from him going through some paperwork. As soon as he sees me he starts packing up to leave. I give him a small smile as he walks away which he returns with nothing. Again, I feel that pain in my chest from the rejection.

"Rylee please have a seat", Alpha Zac says to me. I put Nathan in the back of my mind and go to sit in front of Alpha Zac.

"I asked you to come here to talk about the upcoming war. As you know, you are the key to know when Jax may arrive"

I cringe hearing Jax's name but I know what Zac is talking about. Unfortunate our wolves still have a faint mate bond so I may be able to sense him before others can.

I nod my head in understanding so Zac continues to speak.

"Good. We are relying on you to have that advantage. The most important task is to hide Scarlett once you sense him"

"I can do that Alpha Zac" I respond with confidence.

"Alpha Zac I also wanted to talk about moving out of your house and into the pack house."

He looks at me with a confused look so I continue speaking.

"I think Scarlett is holding back in your relationship so maybe if I remove myself she will be more willing to stay in your bedroom"

I see Zac's eyes light up with the idea so I know my idea worked. He agrees right away and starts to arrange a room for me in the pack house, which I also know is where Nathan stays.

I walk out of the office with a smile on my face. A few hours later I got the news that I have a room in the pack house. I head to the Alpha's house to find Scarlett in the kitchen making dinner.

"Hey Scarlett""Hey Rylee!" She screams and gives me a hug which I return back.

"So I have some news. I'm moving into the pack house"

She looks at me with a sad look on her face so I continue talking.

"I've been thinking about it and I think this is best for you and Zac to connect more. I mean you haven't let him mark you yet"

"Ugh I know I know. I've been holding back" Scarlett says quietly

"Scarlett it's okay to go slow. I just don't want to be the one holding you back."

Scarlett looks up to me with a smile and thanks me for pushing her to be closer to her mate. I stay to help her cook dinner and catch up on everything.

After I pack the few belongings I have, I head to the pack house to find the room I am sharing with two other girls. Thankfully they are friendly and willing to share the room with me.

Around 9pm I head to the forest and walk to the usual pond area to meet Adrian like I have done every night this week. A few moments like I see him walking towards me looking more tired than usual.

"Hey" I greet him with some excitement. He just grunts at me with some greeting.

"Are you okay? If you're not up to train tonight we done have to" I tell him bluntly.

He sighs heavily and runs his hand through his hair.

"I'm just having a shit day" he explains.

"That's fine. We can try again tomorrow" I try to be comforting. I start to walk away to give him some space.

"Wait Rylee. I still haven't had dinner yet. Want to join me somewhere in town?"

Glad he's being friendly again, I happily join him into town to one of the nearest restaurants. As we sit down waiting for our food, I notice how comfortable I am with Adrian even though he is an alpha.

"So are you nervous about Jax starting a war", Adrian asks me.

"I mostly just want to see him dead" I respond back seriously. Adrian gives me a serious look back and nods with understanding.

"Do you believe in the second chance mates" he asks me.

I'm thrown off by his question wondering if he knows about my situation with Jax and Nathan. I suddenly feel nervous thinking about it what to answer without revealing my secret.

Adrian senses my nerves because he reaches out to hold my hand on the table. Surprisingly his touch is calming.

"Promise this will be a secret between us" I hold up my pinky fingered and make him do a childish pinky promise which we both laugh at.

"I've actually already met my mate and then second chance mate", I whisper to him. I look up to his face to see an angry look which I don't understand.

I continue on, "My first mate rejected me for another girl. I think second mate rejected me because he didn't want to commit to someone else after his first mate died"

"Damn" I hear him say under his breathe.

After several long moments of silence, Adrian finally speaks up. "Rylee, you know you're amazing right?"

I look at him with a surprised look not knowing he thought highly of me.

He continues speaking, "Whoever your mates are, they don't deserve you"

I feel some relief from his words and go to give him a big hug. He's shocked at first but then returns my hug which I am happy about.

I start to change the subject not wanting to discuss this even more incase I slip up on who my mates are.

We finish dinner and head back to the pack house. I go to my new room to get ready for bed feeling happy for once that I confided with a friend. ———————————————————————————The next couple days to by normally. Adrian and I continue our training. He hasn't asked me any more mate questions which I am happy about.

Now that I'm staying at the pack house I have seen Nathan more often but usually in a group setting. I always make sure to say hi or smile. So far he hasn't warmed up to me which hurts a little more every night.

I receive a text from Scarlett to come meet her in the Alpha's house. Usually werewolves don't keep phones on them because it could be destroyed if we ever have to go into battle. Thankfully I was in my room when she texted me so I reply that I will be there very soon.

Once I arrive to the house Scarlett opens the door with a glow and big smile on her face.

"Omg you guys mates!" I scream out with excitement as I see the bit mark on her neck.

Scarlett tells me how it all happened. I try to join her excitement as much as possible but I still feel that emptiness in my chest knowing I didn't get the same outcome from my mates.

Scarlett's happiness feels contagious so I head back to the pack house with some encouragement. I decide to test my luck and go to knock on Nathan's door.

Nathan opens the door with a calm face but when he sees me it turns angry. I try not to let that get to me and keep a smile on my face.

"Hey can I please come in. I need to talk to you"

"No" he answers quickly.

"Nathan please. Just this time and then I'll never both you again"

He thinks about it for a minute and then opens the door to let me in.

"Make it quick" he growls at me.

I take a deep breathe and let Scarlett's happiness give me courage for what I'm about to do.

I take a few steps to get closer to Nathan. In the next second I quickly throw my hands around him and smash my lips onto his.

Chapter 6

Once I land my lips on his I start realizing that this is my first kiss so I don't know what I'm doing. A quick moment after, I feel Nathan moves his lips against mine and his hands slide around my back.

I try to hold back my smile and follow his lead with the kiss. It feels amazing and I know my wolf is very happy right now. I lose track of time during the kiss but then I feel myself being slammed into a wall very roughly. I look up to see Nathan on the other side of the room shaking with anger.

My body feels extremely sore from the impact and I feel blood dripping down my head from hitting the wall too hard.

"Don't ever do that again" he growls out

"But you were kissing me back" I agree back weakly while I slowly try to stand up.

"That was a mistake.", he says while walking towards me. I cower in fear from his eyes that have turned black. He moves has hand around my neck and starts choking me against the wall. I start clawing at his arm in fear that he is going to snap my neck.

"Don't ever come near me again" he yells each word out while continuing to chock me. My eyes water from the pain but I try to nod my head in understanding. My wolf howls in pain our mate has given us.

Nathan lets go of my neck which makes me fall down on the floor. I quickly bring myself up wanting to get away from him as fast as possible. As I scramble to the door I turn around one last time to see Nathan starting at me with no emotions.

"I accept your rejection", I whisper while I feel the tears fall down my face. Once I close Nathan's door, I feel my body start to shut down from the overwhelming hurt. I quickly stumble outside to be alone in the forest.

I head to the pond which has become a comfort spot for me. I lay down on the cold floor feeling the effects of my second rejection. My wolf shrinks in fear and none of my injuries are healing.

I know my back is bruised and I have a cut on my head. I touch my neck to also find it very swollen and bruised. I start sobbing until I fall asleep in the forest.

I wake up feeling someone pick me up bridal style. I open my eyes fully and see that Adrian is the one who is carrying me.

"Adrian", I can barely whisper out because of my bruised neck.

"Keep sleeping Rylee. You need rest"

I nod my head and do as he says. I feel my wolf at peace knowing we full trust Adrian.

I wake up again on a bed this time. I look around not familiar with the room I am in. I find a glass of water and pain meds on the stand next to me which I gladly take.

When I lay back on the bed I remember that Adrian picked me up from the forest. When I look around the room again I do realize it does smell that Adrian too. I start crying again wondering when my life turned into a sad story.

I wipe my tears away harshly not wanting to cry over my pathetic mates any longer. I start to get up and clean my face which is when Adrian walks in.

"Rylee you need to be resting", he immediately comes to me and gently pushes me back on the bed.

"Adrian I'm fine." I laugh lightly while he pushes me down to rest.

He smiles at me and just shakes his head in disbelief. He comes sits next to me but this time with a serious expression.

"Who hurt you?", he questions me.

"I accepted the rejection from my second mate", I say quietly making sure I told spill any names.

He looks at me angrily, "If he's hurting you then I need to know who it is"

"He hurt me because I tried to make a move on him. As long as I avoid him he won't hurt me. And I'm planning to leave as soon as this war is over"

"Where would you go"

"Back to my pack with Alpha Sam" I say with a shrug. I'm not very happy with that idea since I know I won't be coming back with the same skills.

I turn my head and see Adrian thinking deeply about something.

"Join my pack", he aggressively states.

"Really?", I ask with raised eyebrows, "you know I'm not strong enough to be a warrior anymore"

"But you're smart as hell and you're still strong enough to train. I want you in my pack", he walks over to me and holds both my hands in his. The feeling seems very intimate but I have become very comfortable with Adrian in this short time.

"Okay I'll do it", I say with a smile. He returns my smile and drops my hands to give me a hug.

"If anyone dares to touch you again, you better tell me" he whispers in my ear. My wolf feels happy in his arms and I start to feel my body heal at a faster rate.

Adrian and I head out together to go through our usually training and meetings for the day. I decide I need to find Scarlett to explain to her that I'm not planning to stay here after the war is over.

I head to Alpha's Zac house but don't find her anywhere. After asking around I find out she's at the orphanage so I start heading there. Once I arrive I see Zac, Scarlett, and Nathan all there to support one of the children that was going through his first shift. I stop at the door and start to shake in fear from seeing Nathan.

While I try to walk out Scarlett notices me and calls my name. I attempt to act calm while my wolf is cowers in fear from being near Nathan.

"Hey Scarlett, can we chat over here real quick"

Scarlett agrees without question and follows me into the kitchen.

"I just wanted you to be the first to know that I'm joining the Crimson Pack once the war is over"

"What do you mean? Zac said you are always welcome to stay here"

"I know I know. I just think I need to try something different and Alpha Adrian is allowing me to join his pack"

"Alright I understand, I will just miss you a lot" , she says before giving me a hug.

"I'm sure we will see a lot of each other since the packs have an alliance. Just remember you are great at being a Luna", I comfort here.

Scarlett and I stay in the kitchen a bit longer to talk about her Luna duties. In the middle of her story I feel a strong pain in my chest which makes me fall over.

"Rylee, what's wrong!"

I take a few deep breathes and feel my wolf sensing something. My mind goes cloudy and I'm unable to hear anything while I see Scarlett and Zac try to talk to me.

After a few moments of panic I finally have a clear mind and feel the panic from my wolf.

"He's coming", I quietly say to Zac since he knows what I'm referring to.

Zac goes into alpha mode and takes Scarlett away to protect her. I then see Nathan looking at me with a confused expression. I close my eyes and quickly get back on my feet to get away from him.

I run out of the orphanage to get to the pack house. Once I get there I see Zac has already started to get everyone in place to prepare for the attack.

Adrian walks over to me and gives me a reassuring smile. I smile back knowing how much I trust him.

Once Zac starts barking orders I snap back into focus and start following the plan we have discussed during the past few weeks. I head to the prison building which is where we decided to keep Scarlett since it was the most protected area.

I stop by to make sure she is doing okay. She seems kind of panicked but I try to calm her down for a bit. After some time I head out again to go to the pack house to collect silver weapons that we made and distribute them to the Crimson Pack warriors.

I see Liam racing up to me looking worried. "Rylee are you doing okay? I heard you sensed him"

"I will be doing great once this man is dead", I say casually not wanting to look weak in front of Liam.

"No one expects you to be brave you know. I just want to make sure you don't push yourself too far", he tells me kindly.

"Thank you Liam. I know the plan. I am going to stay low and assist where needed. I'll be careful"

I give Liam a hug to reassure him. We have been fighting along side for so long it's going to be weird to not be next to him tonight.

The house cleans out once everyone grabs the supplies they need. I do as I promised and stay near the house. I start walking outside just to hear if anything is going on yet.

Almost one hour later is when I start to hear growling in the distance. Another hour later is when I hear the full fight going on. I decide to step a little deeper into the forest until I finally see several groups of wolves fighting one another. To my right I see a few people in human form using silver weapons to attack. I move quietly to the left which is where I see the larger wolves which must be deltas and betas fighting each other.

It seems Jax must either formed an alliance with another pack or convinced rouges to fight with him based on the number of wolves I see. As I tip toe around tress, I get knocked down by a brown wolf but quickly grab out my knife to stab them.

I push him off of me and start climbing a tree to get a better view of everyone. After a few moments my wolf finally senses Jax's wolf who was fighting with Zac's wolf. Jax was currently winning and I didn't see anyone else available to help him.

I think back to my warrior training and find the best route to do a sneak attack. I go around a few trees and find myself right behind Jax. This time I see Zac on the side being pulled away by a some of his pack members and Adrian jumped to continue fighting with Jax.

Adrian got a few good bites in but Jax was still overpowering him. I looked around and saw a lot more wolves being injured so I decide to make a move. I jump down from the tree but see notice my body already feel weaker from the brown wolf that attacked me.

I take out my silver blade and throw it right at Jax's leg which makes him howl in pain. I pull out another blade quickly and throw it on the wide of his neck.

Jax whimpers in pain as he falls down but he then extends his paw at me and rips at my thigh. I feel the blood starting to spill out covering my entire leg.

I fall over next to Jax's dying body and start to feel light headed. Adrian changes into human form and runs to put pressure on the cuts.

"Rylee stay awake!", I hear him scream at me. I try to focus on his voice but everything starts to feel blurry.

I then see Zac and Nathan approach me with concern on their face. Adrian asks them to help stop the bleeding.

"Why isn't she healing?", Zac asks with a panic.

When I start to close my eyes, Adrian starts barking orders and picks me up gently.

"Adrian" I try to shout out but it comes as a whisper with my weak state.

"Don't try to talk Rylee, just stay awake"

"Adrian, listen please", I whisper out again. I feel more blood loss so I don't know how much longer I have.

Adrian stops panicking for a moment and looks directly at me, "What is it Rylee?" He asks softly.

"I really wish you were my mate Adrian", I say right before closing my eyes and falling into the darkness.

Chapter 7

I start to blink my eyes open and look up to see a white ceiling. I try to move my body but everything feels sore.

Eventually I'm able to sit up in a hospital bed. I start to hear voices outside my door but I can't make out what they are saying. Finally someone wearing a white coat walks in introducing themselves as the pack doctor. He says my vitals are looking good but I will still be weak for a couple more days due to the blood loss. He also informs me it's been 12 hours since I blacked out.

"Is anyone here to see me?", I ask him.

"Yes a few people but I advised them it's better to wait a little longer.", the doctor replies back

"Can I just talk to one person? If Scarlett is out there I would really like to talk

I see him walk out and hear him say a few words to the people outside. I then hear some arguing but eventually Scarlett walks into my room with tears in her eyes.

She runs up to me and we both give each other a big hug.

"Are you hurt at all", I ask her right away

"I'm fine Rylee. I've been concerned about you!"

"Don't worry, I feel great" I laugh trying to lighten the mood.

"So Adrian seems very impatient to see you" she tells me with curiosity.

"Really?" I question her. I do remember the last thing I said to him and I feel kind of embarrassed about it now. I know he will eventually find his own mate so I hope I didn't ruin our friendship.

A few hours of rest I wake up again from the sound of the door being opened. Looking outside it seems like it's the middle of the night. I look to the door and see Adrian sneaking in. I start to sit up with a smile on my face.

"Adrian, what are you doing here?" I whisper at him playfully.

"I just needed to know you were okay", he answers me with a serious look.

"Yes I'm okay. Thank you for saving me" I say shyly.

Adrian looks at me with a serious expression while holding my hand until I fall back asleep. By the time I wake up again he is gone.

Scarlett is there when I exit the hospital and start walking back to the pack house. I notice a lot of people are staring at us oddly.

"Everyone knows you defeated Jax. They admire your strength", Scarlett explains to me. I start to blush and look down for the remainder of the walk.

"Zac said to meet him in his office if you're up for it", Scarlett tells me as we enter the pack house. I nod my head and start following her in that direction.

When we walk in I see Zac, Nathan, Adrian, and his beta Grayson. Scarlett runs towards Zac to give him a hug and sit on his lap. I smile at their happiness.

"How are you feeling?", Nathan asks me in front of everyone. I don't dare to look at him since my wolf still shakes in fear around him.

"I-I'm doing great", I answer back while looking away from him.

"Is it true you want to join the Crimson Pack?", Zac asks me. I look over to Adrian gives me a small smile.

"Yes, that is what I have chosen to do"

"Very well, just know you are always welcome back here", Zac replies. I look over to Nathan for a brief second who is glaring at Adrian. At that moment I know I have no intention on coming back for Nathan.

"Let's get going", Adrian tells me while standing up and walking me out of the office.

I quickly pack up my few belongings and say goodbye to some of the pack members that are around. Scarlett gives me a big hug and starts crying which is when I hand her back to Zac to comfort here.

As I turn to leave down the hallway, Nathan walks in front of me which I flinch back from. My anxiety increases not knowing what he intends to do. I take a deep breathe while he leans towards me and gives quick hug.

When I don't return the hug he whispers in my ear, "Goodbye". Not knowing how to react, I just nod my head and continue walking out of the house. At this point I knew even if Nathan would want me back I could never be with him.

I see Adrian and his other warriors packing up into the cars. Adrian guides me over to the car he's driving which I gladly get inside. Once we start driving I notice it's only us two in the car.

While we fall into a comfortable silence I start to close my eyes to rest for the long drive.

"I know Nathan is one of your mates", Adrian says casually. I immediately sit up straight feeling nervous that he knows.

"How do you know?", I ask nervously.

"You we're acting nervous around him and he was giving me a deathly look when I told him you're moving to my pack"

I stay silent, unsure of what to respond.

"Rylee, I won't let him hurt you again", Adrian says to me and then moves his hand to place over mine.

"I'm still scared of him" I admit.

"Would you go back to him if he changed?"

"No, I don't think I could ever forget what he did to me"

"Good", was the last thing Adrian said to me before I fell asleep while holding his hand.

"We're here Rylee", Adrian tells me while shaking me awake.

I jump out of my seat and look around the Crimson Pack. All the buildings are much larger than I've ever seen. I start following Adrian and the others to the pack house.

"I have a small house near the pack house. Since we don't have any space ready in the pack house you will have to stay with me", Adrian explains to me. I nod in understand, still excited to be part of this new pack.

I follow Adrian into his house and he shows me the spare bedroom that I can stay in.

"I'm just next door if you need anything. And feel free to use the kitchen and TV room"

"Thanks Adrian" I say before giving him a hug. He returns the hug and holds me even tighter than usual but I appreciate the comfort.

I go to my new bedroom and start getting ready for bed. As I lay down I feel that familiar emptiness in my chest now that Jax is dead and I'm far away from Nathan. I start to think about how I'm supposed to live my life mateless. I feel my eyes water but I try to tell myself not to cry over these pathetic men.

The first person I think of for support is Adrian. He has helped me so much without even realizing it. I know it's not fair to get close to him since he has his own mate out there but I can't help myself when I tip toe out of my room and knock on his bedroom door.

He opens the door with only a pair of shorts on. I try not to blush while looking at his hard chest and abs.

"Rylee what's wrong?"

"Uh.. I just didn't want to be alone", I quietly say knowing I sound like a child. Adrian opens the door to let me. I give him a small smile and make myself comfortable in his bed.

I feel Adrian slide in next to me. My wolf is at ease now knowing Adrian is next to us. As I start to fall asleep I feel Adrian move his hand around my waist and pulls me closer to his chest.

When I feel the warmth of his skin on mine I easily go into a deep sleep.

Chapter 8

"You're going to need more clothes", Adrian says to me one day over breakfast. I've been fitting into the pack pretty great but I have been running out of clean clothes which forces me to wear his shirts. I secretly love smelling like him but I know I need to get my own stuff eventually.

"I can go out shopping today. Where's the nearest mall?"

"I can take you", he replies.

"Don't you have super important Alpha duties?", I tease him

"Yes, and one of them is to protect my clothes from you", he playfully teases me back.

A few hours later we get ready to head to the mall. Adrian invited his beta Grayson and his mate Lexi to join us.

I haven't had a chance to bond with Lexi very much so I was glad she was coming. Lexi and I dashed to many stores and started our shopping spree while leaving the boys to wonder.

After many shopping bags later, we decided to slow down and look for the boys.

"Hey Lexi, has Adrian been searching for his mate", I felt very nervous about asking this but I figured this would be the best time to do so.

"He used to but his search kind of slowed down sometime last year. No one really asks him about it anymore"

I nod my head in understanding and decided not to push it anymore. I figured Lexi already knew about my rejected mate situation since she never asked me.

We finally find Adrian and Grayson walking around looking lost.

"Anyone hungry?", I ask which Adrian eagerly agreed to. Grayson and Lexi said they have to leave since they had dinner plans with Grayson's parents who live nearby.

I suggested to eat at the pack house since Grayson and Lexi left us but Adrian insisted on staying in town. He picked a nice Italian restaurant which was owned by one of his pack members so we were able to be seated right away.

"So how do you like your new pack" Adrian asks me once we were seated and ordered drinks.

"I have to say it's one of the bests I've been to" I replied which made him smile.

"So I was thinking since I don't have the strength to be a warrior that I could help manage the orphanage."

Adrian gives me a curious look which I figure he would. Usually the orphanages are managed by women that have lost their mates in battle and it was also the role of the Luna to help take care of the kids of the pack.

"I think that would be good but I would still like to train with you"

"Really?" I reply shocked.

"Yes, Rylee. I think you are very talented even without your full strength", Adrian says with another smile. I look down and take a sip of my drink trying to control the blush on my face.

After finishing two cocktails I start to realize that I am feeling kind of drunk. Usually werewolves need a lot more to drink.

"Uh do you feel funny" I ask Adrian and then start to giggle.

"I feel fine but I think the alcohol is getting to you" he says with a concerned face.

"You're cute" I blurt out and then feel my face turn red

"Uh no I didn't mean that" I say while keeping my face low and trying to control the dizziness in my head.

Adrian just starts laughing and then helps me stand up while leaving the restaurant. Once we get back in his car I start to close by eyes feeling sleepy.

"Can I sleep here" I ask with a giggle feeling very relaxed.

"Sure, I can carry you inside" he says while helping to buckle my seat.

"Once you find your mate I will have to move out right" I say with a pout. I turn to look at Adrian but everything is blurry.

"You don't have to worry about that Rylee", he quietly says. I feel his hand on my face helping me move my hair back. His skin feels so good I think I let out a moan.

"Sometimes I hope you won't ever find her so I can stay with you forever", I quietly say before I close my eyes. I feel a pair

of lips kiss my cheek but I don't know if I imagined it or not.
————————————————————————————

I wake up the next morning with the sun shining in my face. I look around and realize I'm in Adrian's room alone. I've slept in his room a few times so I figured he carried me to his bed after I fell asleep in his car.

The memories from last night are kind of blurry but I hope I didn't embarrass myself too much. I make a mental note to never drink in front of Adrian again.

As I get ready to go downstairs I decide to be more formal with Adrian. I don't want to make him feel weird around me and I especially don't want to be kicked out if his future mate knows how close our friendship is.

"Good morning Alpha Adrian", I say to him while he is cooking in the kitchen. He turns to me to give me a weird look.

"I am going to the orphanage to help with breakfast" I say quickly while running out of the house before he can respond.

Once I make it to the orphanage I start helping the workers to make breakfast and clean up after all the children. Only a short while later I see Adrian come inside and greet everyone. My eyes widen in surprise while I try to remain calm around him.

"Need any help in here Rylee", Adrian asks me by sneaking up behind me. I yelp quietly in surprise and playfully slap his shoulder for scaring me.

"What are you doing here Adrian?"

"Well as you greeted me today, I am the Alpha and do like checking up on my pack members", he responds with a big smile on his face.

Thankfully at that moment a little girl ran up to me asking to help brush her hair . I took that as my advantage to escape Adrian and take her to the girls bathroom.

By the time I came out I notice Adrian already left. I knew my reaction around him means something but I try to push it away since I know it's wrong.

I head to the pack house to find Hannah who i learned is in charge of the housing. After asking around I finally find her in one of the offices.

"Hey Hannah, I am -"

"Rylee of course. I have heard about your role defeating Alpha Jax.

"Oh thank you" I say shyly, "I just wanted to ask if any housing available yet"

"Oh yes, we always have something available for females. Especially from the last war, many people found their mates and moved to other packs."

"So you've had room since right after the war"

She nods her head yes and shows me all the available rooms. I think back to when Adrian told me nothing was available so that's why I've been staying at his house.

I tell Hannah I'll be back soon to make arrangements.

I start traveling back to Adrian's house but he's no where to be found. I check the pack house and all his offices but again no luck. After a few moments of frustration I realized there is one place I haven't looked yet.

As I start to trade into the forest I hear some commotion to the right. I lightly walk towards it which is when I see Adrian in wolf form clawing at trees. It looks like he's trying to let some rage out so I watch from the sidelines.

After several moments his wolf starts to settle down and then transform back into human form. When I see Adrian stand completely naked my body starts to heats up. I shamelessly check out every muscle on his body and again curse the moon goddess for not making him my mate.

"Rylee you can come out now"

I jump up, startled by Adrian speaking to me who is now wearing a pair of shorts. I guess I was not as sneaky as I thought I was.

"Sorry I-uhwas looking for you. And I didn't want to interrupt your rage session"

"I was only doing that because someone pissed me off today" he responded.

"What happened?" I asked concerned

"Well someone I thought I was very close with decided to ignore me today" he replies. Right away I realize he's talking about me.

"Why did you tell me there is no housing available in the pack house." I confront him instantly to shift the conversation

He looks taken back for a second but then stands up fully and towers over me.

"I thought I would be a good friend and not force you into living with a much of girls that all talk about wanting to meet their mates" he says aggressively

I take a step back before responding, "I appreciate that but you didn't have to protect me"

"Rylee what is this really about. Why are you being distant" he says while taking a large step towards me.

I lick my lips in nervousness and continue to step back until I lean against a tree. I take a deep breathe and say what I've been meaning to say to him.

"It's not fair to your future mate to be close to another girl. She's going to hate me and force me out of the pack"

I feel Adrian push me further against the tree. He is towers over me and places his hands on my wrists. Before I can ask what he's doing, he grabs my wrists and places them above my head. In the next second he slams his lips on mine and deepens the kiss. I close my eyes in bliss and kiss him back hard while pressing my body against his.

Chapter 9

Adrian moves his hands to my ass and lifts me up against the tree. I wrap my legs around his waist and squeeze my body closer to his. Adrian kisses down my neck which makes me moan out loud.

I feel Adrian's hardness pressed against me. He lifts his head and looks down at my face searching for consent. I think back to all the times fate has screwed me over in the past. I decide in this moment that I want to do something selfish.

I nod my head which is all Adrian needed to bring his lips back to mine and continues to seduce me. He tears my shirt off and starts to touch my bare skin. I kiss him back with eagerness and scratch down his back with passion.

I move my hands down to his jeans to unbutton them. In the same moment I hear a growl behind us. Adrian immediately puts me down and pushes me behind him.

"Stay here", he demands before running towards the direction of the wolf.

I look down and notice I'm missing my shirt so I decide to take off the rest of my clothes and transform into my wolf. I quietly follow the same direction Adrian ran off to.

Eventually I find Adrian on the border of the pack territory on top of a light brown wolf. The lone wolf doesn't seem to fight back, he actually seems scared. I keep hidden behind a large tree while I watch Adrian demand the lone wolf to transform into his human form. Eventually he does and I see the young man looking beaten up and weak.

Surprisingly I see Adrian help him up and find him clothes in a near by basket that is left out around the forest for any pack member to use. Once they are out of sight I transform back into human form and also pick up some clothes from the basket.

I walk through the forest back to the pack house thinking about how I almost let Adrian take my virginity.

"UGH" I scream out loud, feeling frustrated about my life.

I decide to give Scarlett a take my mind off thing. She tells me how romantic Zac is and how life has been great with him. I smile during the phone call, happy to hear everything is going well. My smile drops soon after once she mentions Nathan.

"Zac was having a hard time working with Nathan after the war for some reason. But I think it's going well now, especially since him and Julia have started to date", Scarlett tells me over the phone.

"Julia?" I question in shock.

"Yeah Julia. Weren't you friends with her? She's pretty cool and has always had a thing for Nathan so I'm happy for them. I think it's good for him to move on since his mate passed away"

I take a deep breathe trying to not let my eyes get watery. I quickly end the call with Scarlet not wanting to hear more about Nathan dating Julia.

I find myself taking a walk to clear my head. Soon after I see Lexi running to me saying Adrian wants to meet me at his house.

I decide to be brace and walk into Adrian's house and finding him pacing in the living room.

"Rylee", he says my name before walking up to me and touching my arm in relief.

"What happened with that wolf?" I ask him

"He says his name is Cody and he ran away from a group of hunters that tried to kill him. He's was forced to be a rouge and was just scared", Adrian says while running his hand through his hair.

"Do you believe him?"

"I'm not sure yet. He's at the hospital now. Once he fully heals I will question him again"

When I look back to Adrian I notice he is staring at me intensely. I lick my lips nervously feeling frozen in this spot. He leans towards my face and moves his hand to touch my cheek.

Before he can lean his face closer to mine I take a step back.

"I can't do this Adrian", I quietly say. I turn back to see he has a confused look on his face.

"You seemed happy when I kissed you earlier", he says seductively

"Adrian, I'm not your mate", I say bluntly feeling my skin heat up from being around him.

I see him raise his fist and punch a nearby table causing it to break. "I know that" he growls out in frustration.

"It's not fair to her" I continue on to push my message. "What happens when you met her? That's not fair to me either!"

I take a breathe after my speech and watch Adrian put his hands in fists and breathing heavily.

After several moments of silence he finally says, "I need to show you something". He walks towards me again and grabs my arm dragging me to the door.

"Where are we going?", I ask in confusion.

He doesn't answer me until we get to his car and opens the passenger door for me. I pull my arm away from him refusing to get inside.

"I'm not going in the car until you tell me where we're going"

"Promise me you will get in the car after I tell you", he holds out his pinky. I roll my eyes at his childish offer but I cross my pinky with his and say I promise.

"I'm taking you to meet my mate", he whispers to me quickly and then pulls my hand to direct me inside the car. I let him pull me inside the car since my body goes into a shock state after hearing that.

Chapter 10

Wwe sit in silence after 45 minutes of driving into town. I can feel Adrian glancing looks at me but I don't have the courage to look back.

Adrian parks in front of a busy restaurant and gets out of the car. I watch him walk to the passenger side and open the door for me.

I cautiously get out of the car, not sensing any other werewolves around here. I follow Adrian inside the restaurant where he asks for a booth. I blindly follow him again to the table and sit down looking very confused. Adrian looks back at me with a nervous stare which doesn't comfort me at all.

Our waiter stops by to drop off some waters and Adrian orders something for both of us since I remain quiet. Just as I lose my patience I sense Adrian's heart beat accelerate. I see his head turn to the left so I follow his stare to watch a very attractive blonde woman approaching us. She is dressed in a business casual outfit but still has the restaurant brand on his shirt so I assume she is a manger.

She smiles brightly at Adrian who returns a smile back at her. I feel a tinge of jealously from their interaction but I lean back into my chair pretending to be invisible.

"Adrian! It's so nice to see you again", the blond woman says while leaning down to give him a hug.

"Natalia", Adrian greets her while returning her hug. I catch a glance at Adrian's eyes and see affection towards her. I take a deep breathe now understanding that this woman is his mate. His human mate.

"How has Lucy been?", Adrian asks her.

"Oh she's growing up so fast. Already starting first grade", Natalia pulls out her phone and shows him pictures.

I snap out of my shock and observe her hands which is when I spot a diamond wedding band. His human mate is married and has a kid.

I look back to Adrian to see that is he looking right at me. "Natalia I want to introduce you to my girlfriend, Rylee".

My eyes widen in surprise but faking a smile and greeting Natalia.

"Oh my gosh. I am so happy for you guys. ", she says to me while leaning down to give me a small hug.

She turns back to Adrian to say her goodbyes and then walks away. I turn back to give her another glance, still not believing what just happened.

"Her husband owns this restaurant. I invested in a few places in this town including this restaurant. That's when I found her", Adrian tells me with a faint sadness in his eyes.

After noticing I don't have anything to say he continues, "I tried to get closer to her but I can't be selfish. She's human. She doesn't belong in our world. She already started a family before I found her", he explains his reasons for not pursuing his mate.

I nod my head slowly trying to understand his situation. I look back to Natalia who seems happy with her human life.

"Rylee please say something", Adrian pleads to me.

"I-I'm sorry you can't be with your mate", I finally manage to say. Adrian moves his hand across to table to grab mine. He slowly rubs his thumb across the back of my hand while continue to stare at me.

"Even when I first met Natalia I didn't have that strong mate reaction that everyone talks about. Maybe it's because she's human or maybe it's because I found her at the wrong time"

I try to pull my hand away from his feeling uncomfortable but he squeezes my hand even harder.

"Rylee I want to be with you. I feel a connection with you and I know you feel it too", Adrian whispers to me.

"What are you going to tell the pack?", I ask him thinking how it can look to mate with someone who's not your real true mate.

"I will tell them I didn't have luck with my mate so I decide to chose my own. If they aren't happy with their Luna then they can leave"

I feel my skin heating up from his touch after he mentions Luna. I lick my lips from my nervous habit. I hear Adrian let out a low growl towards me.

"Don't do that in public Rylee. I can barely hold from touching you right now"

This time I manage to pull my hand out of his, not used to feeling this turned on. I look back at Adrian and see a smirk on his face.

I quickly change the subject to our training plans which helps ease the tension. We finish our meals and head outside. On the way we pass Natalia who is standing by a tall handsome man who I assume is his husband.

Adrian approaches him as a friend and gives him a hug. Natalia also gives us both a final hug before leaving. I look back to Adrian who places his hand on my lower back as he guides me to his car feeling confident.

It is strange Adrian doesn't seem jealous around his mate's husbands. Maybe he is telling the truth that their bond isn't as strong as it's supposed to be.

I have heard myths of human mates but never met one before. I look over Adrian who is not driving out of this town and think why he would be paired with a human mate instead of a werwolf. I start to doze off thinking of all the reasons why I wasn't chosen for him.

I slowly open my eyes to see Adrian on my side of the car picking me up from my seat.

"I can walk" I mumble to him. He continues to carry me inside his house without putting me down. I move my hands around his neck and squeeze lightly to show my appreciation.

Once we get to his bedroom he gently lays me on the bed. I start to open my eyes again to see Adrian walk into the bathroom. I get up lazily to take off my clothes and grab one of Adrian's shirts to be more comfortable.

After a few moments I hear the bathroom door open to see a shirtless Adrian walk out. I shamelessly check him out while licking my lips. I see his eyes turn darker and move toward me on the bed.

He grabs my face and pulls me into a deep kiss. He moves his hands to my sides and lays me on the bed. I moan into his mouth letting myself into his touch.

He lifts his head and continues to kiss down my neck. I roll my eyes back and moan lowly from the feeling of his lips all over my skin.

"Adrian can we take it slow" I shout out before he tries to kiss me again.

Adrian lets out a sigh and then moves himself to lie next to me on the bed. I bit my lip feeling pathetic for disappointing him. Just as I begin to get off the bed I feel Adrian wrap his arms around my waist and pull me closer to him.

I try to move my body to get more comfortable but Adrian squeezes my waist to keep me from moving.

"I suggest you don't move unless you want me on top of you again", he whispers into my ear before kissing me neck.

I feel a smile take over my face and then relax into Adrian's arm not daring to move against him again.

Chapter 11

I feel Adrian's hard body against mine as I stir awake the next morning. My body heat up and start moving my hands on his chest.

I lick my lips liking how close our bodies are. The next second I feel Adrian move on top of me. He grabs my wrists and places them above my head so I can't move.

I feel his hardness rub against my lower stomach as he places kisses down my neck. I moan in satisfaction and wrap my legs around his waist. I start grinding against him so his hardness rubs against my core.

I feel Adrian's body tense up as I continue to move my body against him.

"Rylee behave yourself before my wolf takes over", he growls into my ear.

"I don't care anymore Adrian" I say out of frustration before kissing him.

Adrian growls into my mouth but deepens the kiss. I continue to squeeze my legs around him and moan into his mouth. He moves one of his to explore the rest of my body.

After a minute of pure bliss, Adrian abruptly stops and jumps off of the bed. I breath heavily confused by the sudden coldness. Adrian doesn't even glance at my direction as he angrily walks into the bathroom.

I embarrassingly run out of his room as fast as possible trying to not let my tears fall from the rejection.

Once I'm back in the pack house I take a shower to scrubs off Adrian's scent from my body. I don't want any pack members asking why I smell like their alpha especially after he left me in is bed.

I spend the rest of the day training with other female pack members hoping to get my mind off everything.

I bond really well with Lexi, the Beta's mate, but I have a feeling she is told to make me feel welcome. Thinking of all my bad luck I decide to enjoy hanging out with Lexi and her friends.

We decide to go to the pack house for dinner which is the first time I sense Adrian around all day. I take a deep breathe trying be best to ignore him knowing how much he affects me.

As I wait in line for the buffet I feel his presence right behind but but he doesn't say a word. I look around for Lexi and see she is with Grayson who has also joined the line near us.

I collect my food and walk to the farthest empty table. Adrian decides to right next me while I uncomfortable begin to eat my food. The next moment I feel his warm hand on my thigh squeezing gently.

I try to move my leg from him but then he squeezes harder and lets out a growl. Eventually Grayson and Lexi also join the table so I decide not to make a scene.

I try to act like his touch does not affect me until Adrian leans into my ear to whisper, "you're making it very hard to take it slow"

I bit my lip not being able to control myself anymore. I abruptly stand up from the table and say a quick goodbye to Lexi.

I quickly walk out of the pack house and into the forest to let out some steam. As I turn left I run into someone who throws me over their shoulder. I start kicking and screaming until I realize the man is Adrian.

"Adrian put me down" I scream out while continuing to kick my legs. He continues to carry me through the forest without saying a word.

Finally I feel him stop moving and about to put me down. As I think my feet are about to hit the ground I feel my whole body submerge into water again. Panicked, I swim to the top of the lake until my head pops up and I can breath.

The next moment I see a shirtless Adrian jump into the lake right next to me. Feeling extremely angry I start swimming out of the lake until Adrian grabs my waist under the water.

"Adrian stop it!" I yell while slapping his shoulder.

Adrian manages to grab my waist and lift me up against him. Out of habit I move my legs around his waist and hold onto his shoulder. Adrian puts his hand behind my neck so I look into his eyes.

I feel my heart stop when I look directly into his eyes. I squirm against his hold not liking how easily he can affect me.

"Rylee stop fighting this", Adrian says while continuing to rub my neck slowly.

"You left me this morning", I reply quietly

"My wolf was about to take over. You said you want to take it slow so I'm going to"

"I changed my mind" I reply bravely

"Rylee this is too important to me to mess up"

I try to hold back a smile and realize that's exactly what I needed to hear.

I move my hands around his neck and pull him into a kiss. He immediately responds and deepens the kiss.

I tug at his hair to lift his head.

"Adrian I'm ready" I whisper before kissing him again and tightening my legs.

Adrian move his hands to my waist and squeezes roughly. I moan into his mouth and start taking off my shirt.

Adrian slams me against the dock and helps me take off my clothes. At the same time I reach down to take his shorts off and feel how hard he was.

"Rylee please be absolutely sure before I lose control", he growls into my ear before kissing down my neck.

I move my hand to his hardness again to prove my point. Adrian moves his hands to my ass and lifts me up so I'm aligned with him.

I lower myself onto him slowly while moaning loudly. Adrian slams himself into me while kissing and licking my neck. I move my neck back so he has better access to while he continues to move inside of me.

I push my breasts out to get a better angle making Adrian lower his mouth to suck on my breasts. I move my hands to his back and scratch down aggressively liking the pleasure of pain.

I start to moan louder as I get closer to my climax. Adrian lowers his hand to rub my clit until I reach my organism.

Adrian continues to move inside of me faster knowing he is getting close.

"Don't finish inside of me" I moan out while Adrian roughly grabs onto my hips. I feel Adrian kiss my neck again and expose his sharp teeth.

"Adrian" I moan out as a warning as he continues to nip at me.

Adrian turns me around so I'm facing the dock. He renters me from behind. I moan loudly from the different position.

I hold onto the edge of the dock to keep my balance as Adrian continues grabs my waist to move inside of me. He moves one of his hands back to my clit until we both reach a climax.

I lean my head back until my breathing goes back to normal. Adrian continues to hold me tight and slowly kisses my neck.

I turn around slowly and slap Adrian across the face and then quickly jump out of the water and onto the dock.

"I told you not to finish inside of me" I try to say seriously but clearly have a huge smile on my face.

I look back to see Adrian also jumping onto the dock which is the moment I start to run. I heard a loud growl which is when I realize running away from an alpha after slapping him was a very bad plan.

Chapter 12

I turn left quickly through the thick forest. My heart is beating incredible fast but I can't hold back the smile on my face.

I slow down just to transform into my wolf since I was already naked. I start running even faster in wolf form, feeling good that I wasn't caught yet. The excitement quickly dies down when I feel a large wolf jump on top of me from my right.

I roll over and get myself back up to realize the black wolf that jumped on me was Aiden. My wolf instantly wants to obey him but I decide to take control and keep running away. I hear Adrian's wolf growling behind me but I have a feeling he is enjoying the chase.

I get to run for another 30 seconds until Adrian's wolf knocks me over again. This time his paws hold mine down so I couldn't escape again. Knowing I didn't have a chance against an alpha wolf I transformed back into my human form.

I look up and see Adrian has done the same but he is still holding me down with his hands.

He lowers his head so his face is extremely close to mine.

"Listen closely, I will tie you up until you're begging me to finish inside of you me. Don't ever run away from me Rylee"

My heart is pounding even faster than before. I my eyes widen at his vulgarness but I find myself nodding to his words, like I want them to be true.

He leans down and slams his lips against me. I willingly accept his kiss and life my body to be closer to his. Adrian holds me down tighter so I'm not able to move closer to him.

He smirks down at me knowing he has me right when he wants me. He moves his lips down my neck and sucks and licks every inch of my neck and chest. Once he gets to my breasts I start shaking from the frustration.

I fought his hold on my arms even tighter knowing I need him to touch me down there

"Rylee stop, you're gonna hurt yourself" he breaths into my ear while he continues his assault on my neck.

"You know what you have to say" he mumbles into my skin.

I take a deep breath while I feel my wetness increasing. I bit my lip hoping I can muffle my moans hoping he gives up before I do.

Just as I feel myself calming down, Adrian's hardness lightly touching my clit.

"Adrian please" I moan out surprising myself.

Adrian moves his body again so I continue feeling his heavy cock on my stomach.

"Okay I give in. Please" I breathe out

"Say the words Rylee", Adrian growls out knowing he is on the edge too

I turn my face and show him my brown eyes to look directly into his dark green ones.

"Do whatever you want with my body. Finish inside of me or cum on me. I don't care. Just make me feel good"

Adrian lifts my body and slams me to the nearest tree so fast that I feel light headed. His fingers hold up my ass tightly while he slams himself inside of me.

I throw my head back letting out a loud moan that I desperately needed. Adrian continues to mercilessly pound into me while holding me up. I can't even try to match his strokes because they're so incredible fast. Now I realized he was actually going gentle our first time in the lake.

"Adrian!" I scream out as he continues to hit me deep inside building up my climax. He lowers his head to clamp down on breast and suck on nipple. Shortly after I feel my orgasm hit me hard leaving me leaning on Adrian, unable to move.

He slows down a bit and leans against the tree so I have more support for my body. He moves his hand around neck and leans in to give me soft and slow kisses.

My mind is mush right now. I was just fucked by this man and now he's kissing me like I'm a twig.

I move my hands around his neck and move my fingers through his hair and pull hard. He bits my lip even harder and increases his pace inside of me. I lean my head back enjoying the roughness again feeling another build up.

I keep my arms on his shoulders for balance while he squeeze his hand around me neck. I start to lose air but feel myself getting light headed. My body weirdly relaxes from the pressure and I give in to another light orgasm at the same time Adrian growls while releasing himself inside of me. ——————————————————————————————The next morning I find myself back to my normal training schedule. I feel like my wolf has more energy than ever and it feels amazing.

I had to argue with Adrian last night that I wasn't going to be sleeping in his bed every night now. I still wanted to have my own bed in the pack house while we continue whatever this is.

Now that I know what Adrian can do to my body, I was extremely nervous being around him. I still can't believe the first times I had sex were in a lake and against a tree. I try to hold back my smile while remembering those moments.

The thing I can't figure out is why Adrian insisted on finishing inside of me. I thought he just lost control the first time but clearly he was trying to make a point and I wanted to know his true intentions.

During the end of our training I see Cody, that rouge wolf Adrian found the other day. Grayson was holding his hand and walking him towards the prison cell. I know they were waiting for him to heel so now they will question him to make sure he's safe to be around.

Ever since the war with Jax I know everyone's been on edge so all precautions are raised. I study Cody's body language and it shows he scared but corporative which is a good sign.

After dinner I noticed I still haven't seen any sign off Adrian today which seems to bother me. I try to ignore the feeling and take a walk after dinner. I end of near the prison building which gives me an idea to talk to Cody.

I walk inside and see many guards at each door. This was probably the only moment I was grateful I was know as the person who killed Jax since everyone trusted me to go inside.

I didn't get question until I Dylan, Jax's Delta, comes up so me.

"Rylee you shouldn't be here right now" Dylan says to me.

I eye him suspiciously but continue to walk through the hallway. I hear him sigh loudly and follow me. Glad to know he's wasn't gonna try to bother me.

Eventually I hear Adrian's voice which sounds angry. I run towards his voice and find him in a cell with Cody, who's tied up to a chair. It looks like he's already hit Cody a few times in the face.

Adrian turns around instantly once I come into view.

"Rylee you need to leave" he says harshly. I continue walking forward towards Cody who is staring back at me.

"Rylee", Adrian says more softly and grabs my arm to stop me from growing further.

"Adrian I'm not some princess. I've seen worse as a warrior" I remind him. I pull my arm free and continue walking to Cody. I touch the straps on his chair which lightly burn me meaning there is silver twisted into them.

Cody is shaking in his chair clearly scared and uncomfortable.

"What did you find out so far" I turn around and question Adrian and Dylan.

Dylan looks at me in shock and turns to Adrian for help. Adrian turns his hands through his hair and lets out a sigh.

"Not much. He said he lives with some other rouges in a town nearby. He won't say anything about the werewolf hunters he mentioned before"

"Can I try a different method" I ask. Adrian raises his eyes but eventually nods his head knowing he felt defeated after trying all day.

I pull of the straps around his wrists and ankles not bothered by the silver. Cody instantly rubs his wrists to soothe the pain. I grab a water bottle nearby and hand it over to him.

"Adrian can you back up a little bit" as I notice he is hovering over me.

"I'm not moving" he says holding his place.

I roll my eyes and push his body towards the other wall. "He's already scared of you. He needs a new face to talk to now." I whisper to him. Eventually he listens and lets me guide him to the far away wall so he can still see us.

"Fell better" I ask Cody after he finishes the water.

He just nods his head but I see some sparkle back in his eyes.

"Do you have siblings" I ask already feeling Adrian rolls his eyes thinking this is stupid

"Yes, my sister"

"You're lucky then. I wish I had siblings" I smile to him. "Do you think she's worried about you"

"Yes I think so"

"Do you want us to find her and bring her to you"

Cody shakes his head no looking terrified again.

"So you don't want to see your sister" I asked confused.

"I don't want her to come here" I'm he quietly says.

"Why not" I question. I glance towards Adrian who has his arms crossed over his chest and looking intensely at me.

"I wasn't supposed to follow her" Cody says while looking at the ground

"You followed her here"

Cody just shakes his head yes but still doesn't stare at me

"Cody" I say to get his attention

"Why was your sister headed here"

Cody's eyes show fear again so I grab his hand to comfort him. I hear a low growl behind me but ignore it.

"Cody you have to tell me so I can keep you safe"

"They told her to come her to spy"

"The werewolf hunters said this"

Cody shakes his head no. "That's what she told me to say. But I think they're worse than hunters" I see him shiver with fear thinking about these men.

I take a step back figuring that was enough for today and walk towards Adrian and Dylan.

"Can he clean up and get a decent a meal?" I question to Adrian.

"Dylan get someone to help him out. We're still leaving him in the cell though. And get all the warriors together. We need to discuss a lockdown since we have spies now" Adrian rambles on with the guards.

I decide this is a good time to leave the building and head back to the pack house. As I step outside I feel someone pull me back against a wall. Before I can fight back I realize it was Adrian.

"Where do you think you're going" Adrian says while holding my arms down against the wall. I look around realizing people are around making my eyes go wide.

"Adrian not here" I plead. He holds his stare for a few more seconds before letting go.

"Come over tonight" he asks while we walk together towards the houses

"Maybe" I say teasing him. He lets out a small laugh that sounds so sexy.

"Also I wanted to tell you first that I'm going to ask Zac to help look into this spy situation. He was mentioning they may have spotted some rouges near by"

"I think that's a good idea"

"Great, because I was going to ask Zac and Scarlett to also come visit"

I quickly turn to my side and give Adrian a hug which he gladly accepts.

"Really! I get to see Scarlett?" Adrian laughs into my neck and confirms his plan.

I let go of Adrian feeling in high spirits not caring who sees us having a moment.

"But that also might mean he would bring his Beta for protection"

"Nathan?" I whisper quickly turning my happiness into a nightmare.

Chapter 13

It has been 3 days since I heard I might see Nathan again. I've been feeling extreme anxiety from my wolf which has kept me on edge. I've also successfully avoided Adrian too afraid to get closer to him. I didn't fell right that Nathan will be here pretended not to be my mate while I want to be with another man.

One of our pack warriors found me yesterday telling me Adrian wanted to meet in his office. I know he must be livid I never showed up. Scarlet told me they were planning to show up tonight so I figured I would have to talk to Adrian before too make sure he behaves himself.

"Come in", I hear him say right after I knock on his office door. Taking a deep breath I enter his office already seeing him fuming in his chair.

His eyes narrow at me as I casually walk over and sit across from him.

"So I think we need some guidelines starting tonight" I begin to speak. I look up through my eyelashes to see Adrian still staring at me. He doesn't speak so I continue.

"We can't continue this thing between us while Alpha Zac's pack is around for obvious reasons. Actually I was thinking I would just avoid all interactions with visitors and stay in the pack house. Obviously I will just see scarlet separately and...."

I feel my body get picked up from the chair and slammed down on the nearby sofa mid-speech.

"Adrian what the hell!" I scream out from shock.

Before I could say another word I feel his lips on my. I moan into the kiss and run my hands through his hair missing his warmth.

"You drive me crazy", Adrian whispers into my ear while nibbling down my neck.

"I don't like when you ignore me" he continues to bit down on my neck while I moan softly.

"I will punish you soon" he growls out while move his hand to my ass and squeezing hard. I breath hard, suddenly overcome by my body's heat.

Adrian leaves one more heated kiss on my lips before standing both of us and going back to her desk.

"I know your nervous but I won't let anyone hurt you. Ever.", he calmly says while I'm still trying to recover from our intimate moment.

It's close to midnight when we hear the several cars approaching the house. As soon as I spot Scarlet I run over an give me a long needed hug. I was successfully with ignoring everyone else even thought I could feel Nathan who brought Julia with him.

The problem was that I actually liked Julia. I grabbed her and Scarlet over to the house they were staying at to catch up while the men went straight to business.

For the next couple days I thought I deserved an award for my acting. I didn't cringe every time Julia talk about their relationship and didn't flinch when Nathan can close to 10 feet near me. But I wanted to. My body was shaking inside from fear, rejection, and maybe a little disgust.

I went to Adrian every night in secret. He was surprised when I agreed to it but I made sure to sneak it so no one could suspect. I needed the comfort in the arms of the man I love. Yes, I those 2 days I fell in love. Every time Scarlet would share a story of our past I noticed the twinkle in his eyes when he stares at me. I know he timed every gathering to make sure Nathan was not around me.

He cared about me more than anyone else had and I finally noticed it those days. I hated that it still felt wrong. We weren't mates and that scared me more than any other rejection I faced. Alphas are the leaders of their pack which comes with extreme respect. Usually Lunas are welcomed with the same respect and admiration. But I didn't feel strong enough to survive his loss if his pack went against his choice of picking a Luna that was not blessed by the moon goddess for him.

Even with this immense fear I still let myself fall in love with him. As I was walking to the pack house that morning I touched my lips and smiled. Remembering how Adrian was over me in the middle of the night and pleasuring me beyond my dreams.

Scarlet and the pack were set to leave tomorrow which is the same day he said I'm moving packing into his house. I refused immediately thinking he was mad. I was too insecure to share my fear of the packs rejection so I just laughed it off knowing he was plotting something.

I couldn't find Scarlet and Julia around so I decide to take a run before I try again. I was near my favorite lake spot when I ran into him. I feel to the ground and coward in fear. Nathan looked down and gentle picked me back help surprisingly looking remorseful.

"Rylee" if all he growled out before pushing me to the closet tree and started licking and sucking on me neck. I immediately I responded me punching at him, trying to move him off.

He responses were so aggressive that I knew his wolf was taking over. His wolf was mad he rejected his second chance mate and chose to me with another girl. He was trying to take ownership and I was shaking thinking he might lose all control and make me.

The tears let lose knowing I could never overpower him in this stare. Before I could continue to protest I felt the cold air on me again. Shocked, I look up and see Adrian transforming into his wolf on top of Nathan.

Their fight is ugly but I continue to cry knowing I was powerless. Finally Nathan submitted. He turned to look at me in disgust. Like he blamed me for being at the same place and making his wolf lose control. I didn't know if he still wanted to fight this or if he knew he could never win me back.

Adrian let him go with a warning and then ran to me. I let him hug me while I cry into his shoulder. In that moment I found myself healing through him. I couldn't explain it but I knew it was special.

As we were walking back I knew Adrian was bothered I just didn't know why. I surely wasn't ready for what he asked me.

"Did you kiss him?"

I stopped in my tracks and let him see the anger in my eyes.

"He attacked me. Why would it matter if he kissed me if it wasn't consensual"

Adrian let out a long sigh which irritated me even more. "I just need to know how you feel about him now. His wolf is fighting for you"

I slapped Adrian out of reflex. The 2nd time I have slapped an alpha. I felt like that was a sure sign I was insane.

"Yes that changed something. It made me want him even less because he has hurt me again. You think I would want that because it's fate. I stopped believing in fate a long time ago" I spit out before pulling from his hold and running back to the pack house.

I was hurt. I heard him shouting after me but I made sure so be around the pack so he would be distracted. I wanted to sulk in my misery for a little longer before he made it all better. And I knew he would make it better because I loved him. Even though I never admitted that to him.

I found Scarlet and Julia shortly after and continued my great acting abilities and pretended that everything was great. We went shopping as requested and spend an easy day together. I tried my best to be present but it was hopeless everyone Adrian texted me.

I was so distracted in my thoughts that I didn't notice the first sign of an man following us. We had the three pack warriors of each pack guarding us but I still feel guilty for not being alert.

"Scarlet I thought you would go easy on the shopping since you said you do this often" I playfully say, seeing the 10 shopping bags carried by her pack members.

"Zac loves it when I buy stuff for myself" she giggles. My hear warms knowing his happy she is.

We were almost back in our territory when the car in front was hit by a wolf. Our pack warriors instantly fought back at our attacker. But there was too many enemies also approaching our car.

Going to full defense mode I shove Scarlet to one of the warriors and ordered him to take her to safety immediately. I don't even remember which pack he was part of but I'm just thankfully he followed through even with her protests.

I look around and find Julia fighting off other wolves. There was about 10 wolves against Julia, myself, and the remaining five pack warriors.

As soon as I see Julia struggle I go to help her. One of the warriors was also helping Julia knowing he had to save his Beta female. I told him to also take her back but Julia was back to help me.

She had two wolves knock her down when I came over and kicked one of them off. I felt so stupid for not having my silver daggers with me. I always bring them when leaving the territory but I knew I was too distracted today.

I saw 2 warriors fall before I have the order again to take Julia to safety. Finally he noticed we were weakened and oblige. I saw the smaller wolf come behind me which I prepared to punch back but then I felt the wolfsbane being injected in me.

And that leads to the present. Waking up to find myself in a cell surrounded by silver. I spent an hour studying my surroundings to study all possible escapes. I've been in these situations before already knowing I could easily escape. But I chose to stay. I wanted to know who attacks us assuming Scarlet's life is in danger again.

What felt like several hours later is when I heard footsteps coming down the stares. When I saw him is when I knew this was about revenge. Oliver stood in front of the cell looking at me in disgust. He was the younger brother of Jax. Everything knew heard the evil of Jax but I didn't study that much of Oliver.

"I wanted Scarlet to be with me today but I will still be satisfied to slowly torture the one who killed me brother" was the only thing he said to me tonight while someone else tied me to a chair with more silver.

I pretended to scream in pain hoping to please him so he would leave happy. I knew at that moment I was dealing with evilness so I had to plan my escape as soon as possible.

Chapter 14

I stopped trying to keep track of time while I prepare my body to escape from this shack. I still felt the poison in my body that was ejected into me.

I heard light few steps coming close, turning to see a petite girl with light features approaching me with water. She looked extremely familiar to me but I couldn't place my finger in it.

I stayed quiet as she places a bottle of water at my feet clearly confused on how they expected me to drink it. Most likely another torturing tactic.

As she starts to walk away I feel a sudden burst of realization. "Cody" I whisper, knowing she would be able to hear it.

As she turns around I continue whispering knowing time is precious in here.

"I can bring you to Cody. He's scared and he needs you"

"How should I trust you" she whispers back already walking towards me again.

"You can keep my wrists tied in silver rope." I desperately say knowing I'm taking advantage of her frightened state.

"I don't believe you"

"Cody followed you to spy on the Crimson Pack. He accidentally got caught too close to the border but he's alive. He said someone was ordering you to spy at the pack. Now I know that was Oliver. He needs you. He needs his sister"

She looked baffled that I knew so much information but then I saw the moment her switch went to fight mode. She quietly opened up the cage and removed the restraints on me except for 1 silver rope tied around me wrists.

"Leave your phone" I instruct her, "that's the first thing they will track".

I follow her to a busted window and help her climb through even with my tied wrists. I then follow her out without making a sound. I look around and see a dirt road surrounded by trees.

I look to Cody's sister to guide me the right way which she finally does after realizing no one heard us. Once we tip toe a safe distance away we start running at full speed until sunrise.

I stop first finally recognizing my surroundings.

"What are you doing? We have to keep moving"

"What's your name" I ask her as a response, "I never asked for your name.

"Charlie"

"Charlie listen, I'm weak. I still feel the wolfsbane in my blood and you haven't untied my wrists yet. I need to rest. I know a pack nearby that will help me"

Charlie quickly comes to untie my wrists herself. I knew I could have easily done it but I wanted to get her to trust me.

"I'm staying with you until I find Cody", she responds as I lead the way to the Silver River Pack.

Alpha James was a little older than me with a very kind soul. Alpha Sam sent me to work with her pack many times during my training years. They are a smaller pack that stay away from violence but still value strength and training.

I saw the familiar path of white oak trees that lead to large lake that borders most of the pack.

"Are we hear" Charlie asks.

"Almost. We're gonna stay here until they come to us. This is a peaceful pack. I don't like to alarm them"

After a short time I see a pack member approaching us at the other end of the lake. I see he is already rowing a boat to us and explained Alpha James has approved me to cross over.

As soon as I see James I let me body relax knowing I'm safe. I also notice how rundown I am. From my wrists to my feet I feel open scars that still haven't healed. I feel my head pounding and the weight of my eye lids.

"Rylee" I hear him saying but it sounds faint.

"Rylee what happened" he keeps screaming as he runs towards me

Charlie comes near me first to catch my first fall. James came shortly after to fully carry me. I briefly heard Charlie explain our journey until I gave into the darkness. ———————————————————————————I woke up on a soft bed in a room I recognized in Alpha James house that I have stayed at before. There is an IV hooked up to my arm which I carefully remove, already seeing my bruises and cuts healed.

I stand up noticing there is a spare clothes and a towel near the bathroom which I take advantage of and clean the filth off of me. As I rinse myself under the hot water my thoughts go to Adrian. I lightly touch my body pretending to mimic his movements. My thoughts suddenly turn dark thinking of our latest encounter which feels like ages ago.

I start to wonder if a relationship can every work knowing we have our rejected mates around. I feel a tears roll down my eyes as they blend into the water stream.

Even after my small breakdown I just want to run into the only man that has wanted me. Fought for me. Fucked me. Made love to me.

As I dry off and get dressed I start to hear loud voices near by. I quietly open my door to observe the commotion.

"Where the fuck is she?"

"Adrian calm down. James said she's taking care of her and I trust him"

"She has a mate, kind of. Do you think her wolf needs him?", I recognize Zac asking

"That's not her fucking mate. I can help her heal. We have a connection" Adrian growls out.

"My beta followed me here. He said he just needs to see her"

"I think the fair thing to do will be to ask Rylee what she wants. I will be right back"

I hear a growl and then both Zac and Sam shouting out to calm down. I run back into the room talking everything in. The first thing I want to do is see Adrian. And the last thing I want to do is see Nathan.

A moment later Alpha James knocks on the door so I let him in.

"You're looking much better" he smiles to me with his shiny green eyes.

"Thanks to you"

"I'm guessing you heard our little Alpha argument" I laugh lightly at his way to lighten the mood.

"You haven't found your mate yet right?" I ask knowing we have had friendly conversations about our mates before.

"Not yet" he responds with a hint of sadness.

"Before you judge me please understand I tried with my mate. It just didn't...."

"Rylee I would never judge you. I may think Adrian is a bit of a hothead but he definitely loves you"

"Wait you think he loves me" I just up from surprise

James smirks at me, "The man tried to fight me on my own territory to see you. Is it so hard to believe people fall in love with you"

In my head I remind myself that I have been rejected by two mates so yes it is hard to believe. Sometimes I regretted being a warrior because I didn't feel feminine enough. Kind enough. Soft enough. I just wanted someone to admire me for my strength.

I jump into James' arms thanking him for just being his kind self knowing the moon goddess will bless him with his soulmate.

Unfortunately at the same time I hear a pounding at the door and see Adrian walk in with murderous eyes.

"I leave you two alone" James casual says while walking out.

I freeze in place feeling the air thicken around us.

"Rylee", he growls out while stepping forward to me. I squeal once he makes it to me and grabs my thighs to lift me up. I instantly wrap my legs around his waist and my arms around his neck.

He throws me on the bed near by with some force, clearly still angry. He crawls on top of me and grabs my wrists to hold over my head.

"Everyone man needs to know you're mine. Tell me why I shouldn't mark you right here, right now"

"Do it", I whisper. I see a hint of surprise in his eyes not thinking I would agree. "I want you. I want to be selfish and be yours. Mark me right here, right now"

Adrian growls his approval before claiming my lips in a heated kiss. I kiss him back which equal intensity. After he successfully kisses, licks, and sucks my lips until they are perfectly swollen.

My pleasure is short lived once Adrian leaps off the bed. The familiar feeling of rejection hits me strong. I look up to see Adrian breathing heavy with a stressful frown and a painful look of regret.

Chapter 15

I feel a single tear run down my face which I roughly clean off.

"Fuck Rylee, no", Adrian notices my state and tries to get back on the bed. I roughly jump off not wanting to be at his mercy again.

"Rylee come back here"

"Adrian fuck off"

Well that sure pisses him off even more. I feel a rough touch on my waist and then get pulled back against his body. His hand comes around to me front thighs and runs up my dress lightly.

"Stop running from me. I don't like that" he roughly says against my neck and then bits me earlobe.

I fail to stop the moan that escapes my mouth as he continues to rub his hand so close to my delicate area.

"You left me first" I manage to say, remember what got us in this mess.

"I jumped off because I didn't want to mark you when I was angry. That's not fair to you. I'm going to make it special when I make you mine", he continues to nibble down my neck which I give full access to.

My heart jumps back to life knowing he still wants to mark me. I feel like a little girl eating up all his attention on me.

"You drive me crazy" he repeats my thoughts as he finally places his hand to my sweet spot realizing how much he affects me.

I moan out loud, maybe too loud, as he moves his fingers inside me and fondles my breast. With every noise leaving my lips, Adrian increases his pace. I let myself go as soon as Adrian bits into my shoulder.

"I can't believe we just did that in James' house", I say speechlessly.

"He has a soft spot towards you. I don't like it".

I roll my eyes at his Alpha attitude.

"It's called being a kind friend"

"I still don't like it" Adrian mumbles

I clean myself quickly and then follow Adrian out the door. As I see Alpha Zac I instantly remember my panic earlier.

"Is Nathan really here" I squeeze his arm needed any sort of comfort. Adrian sees the fear in my eyes and collects me into his arms.

"He wasn't allowed inside and it will stay that way. I won't let him near you"

I whisper a thank you to him and continue to hold on to his arm as we meet the rest of the group.

Alpha James gives me a knowing look which makes me blush. Alpha Sam gives me a fatherly embrace which I was grateful for. Alpha Zac gives me a sympathetic hug and almost guilty look.

"I can't thank you enough for saving Scarlet. We already talked to Charlie and she gave us the information to find Oliver and his followers" Zac expresses to me.

"I promised Charlie we will take her to see Cody" I look up to Adrian

"I know baby, she's coming with us" I slightly blush at his endearment.

I take a deep breath feeling my confident surging back into me.

"Zac I'm sorry but I don't want to talk to him or even see him" I express knowing I wouldn't have to explain myself.

Zac simple nods his head and confirms he will take care of it as he leaves us.

I give a long goodbye with Alpha Sam and James before we left. Adrian held me close the whole time which both annoyed me and brought me joy. Overall I was exhausted once we left.

"Adrian" I sigh once we're we make it into his car and I lean into his side.

"Go to sleep. I got you" he kisses the top of my head which leaves me with butterflies

"I love you" we're my last thoughts as I drifted off into his warmth.

Chapter 16

I woke up alone but I knew I was in Adrian's bed as soon as I smelled his scent all around me. My body woke me up with an urgent need to feel his skin on mine, feel him inside of me. I was overwhelmed with this heat and also upset he wasn't around to satisfy it.

I start searching for him but surprisingly find Grayson in the kitchen.

"What are you doing here" I ask causally while preparing a glass of water.

Grayson clears his throat nervously which alarms me,"Adrian wanted me to look after you while he had to complete some tasks"

"What kind of tasks"

"The alpha-kind" Grayson shrugs. "Oh and here's your phone. We found it attack site"

I take my phone noticing it has a few new scratches but functions normally. I saw hundreds of texts from Scarlett and Julia which I answered instantly.

I also saw some messages from James which I figured would be better to ignore. Finally I saw a message from Adrian.

I have to work all morning. Grayson will be over. Please stay inside until I'm back.

I pout re-reading the message several times. It could not have been more dry. More unaffectionate it. I couldn't help to use this as an alert that we are not mates. How could we make something last without the same bond. I know my love was real. I felt it in every happy, scared, sad, and heated moment. I felt him, felt myself always wanting him. Like I couldn't remember how it felt before him.

I had a bad feeling and I hated it. My masochist side pushing me to find out what it was even if it was going to hurt.

I manage to convince Grayson that I wanted to call some friends out in the backyard and enjoy the sunlight.

"I can join you"

"I'd rather talk in private. My conversations with Scarlet usually get very detailed" I emphasize which makes him back off not wanting to know more.

I make my way outside and sit on one of the patio chairs for a short time. Eventually I see Grayson distracted on his phone which was my cue to sneak around the house to start searching.

Once I started walking I realized I didn't really have a plan. I just know something felt off and I wanted to find out what it was. I ended up walking to the far south side of the territory. I rarely came to this area before because it was mostly built for the youth. There was several nice parks with even a coffee shop and library used mostly by students.

My heart stopped the moment I saw her golden hair shine in the sunlight. My eyes felt heavy with tears that I managed to hold back. They were sitting at one of the park benches, holding coffee cups, and laughing towards each other. It actually looked perfect. Like a perfect date with two beautiful people.

I couldn't help but notice how gentle Natalia looks. I felt my insides crumble knowing I would never have that look. I've fought too much, too hard to be anything but gentle.

I retrieve my steps back to Adrian's house already knowing my fate. My cruel fate.

Grayson was calling me as soon as I snuck back in the backyard. I opened the door already seeing him panic. He knew.

"Rylee, fuck, where did you go?"

"Save it. I already saw them"

He raises a hand behind his neck looking guilty, "Uh what do you mean?"

I let out a long sigh knowing he doesn't want to betray his alpha so I wasn't trying to get a confession.

"Have you every met someone else with a human mate" I whisper feeling the weight of body give in as a sit on the couch.

Grayson looks pale, confirming I found out the worst, but he quickly recovered and came to sit next to me.

"No I haven't."

"They never rejected each other. That's why she still feels it. Or feels something. It won't ever go away now" I let out while feeling one evil tear escape down my check.

"Rylee it's not like that. I've seen it from the beginning. It's always been different. Only platonic" he tries to comfort me but knowing he shouldn't touch me in this state.

"How does it feel? To be in love with your mate. To be with Lexi"

Grayson couldn't hide the smile on his face once I said her name. It was so powerfully it make me smile back.

"It's hard to describe in words" he simple says.

"That's okay. Your face says it all". I lay back on the couch letting my tears fall down freely. I feel my face form a sad smile while I think of the few memories with Adrian. My heart tells me it's beating deeply for Adrian but my head is doubting if his does the same for me.

I doze off feeling worn out but I'm awoken shortly after hearing Adrian and Grayson's low voices.

"Why the fuck has she been crying"

"Listen man, she must of had a feeling and went to go look for you. It was so quick I didn't even notice it. You know she's trained very well"

"What do you mean she went to look for me. I didn't see her"

"I don't know exactly. But she definitely say something. I didn't tell her any details"

Adrian let's out a few more curse words until Grayson excuses himself from the house. Continuing to look asleep, I feel Adrian pick me up and lay me back on his lap. I feel ashamed enjoying this moment knowing it shouldn't belong to me. My selfishness lets me lay in his arms a bit long while he strokes my hair.

I turn my face towards him and raise myself to his lips. We both fall towards each other until our lips are locked. It's a slow kiss but a meaningful one. I move my body to straddle him and start undressing. I make my needs very clear to him which instigates a fire in his eyes until we are both fully naked.

Looking into his eyes, breathing heavily I lower myself slowly on his hardness. I take my time saving this memory that I will hold forever. Adrian grabs my neck and pulls forward to connect our lips again. This time the kiss is heated, passionate knowing our bodies have taken over.

I move against him at a steady pace knowing it would drive him crazy. He grabs my hips roughly and takes over my movements just the wave I crave. I fall apart feeling myself rubbing on his bare skin while he mouth is still consuming me. I cry out a moan feeling every emotion run through me.

Adrian picks me up and lays me on the couch while still moving inside me. He mouth devours each inch of my neck and chest until I feel another build up. I couldn't use my words. It was too much in that moment to ask for what I needed. Too afraid I was going to reveal to much.

After Adrian was satisfied marking me chest he finally pulled back and thrusted back in the perfect combination of pleasure and pain. His hand moved to my clit to rub lightly enough until my eyes roll back and my legs shake around him. One thrust later he's finishing inside of me, milking every minute and more.

I lay there holding onto to his shoulders, preparing for the inevitable fallout. Adrian slowly moves off of me and even more slowly pulls out while we both let out a moan.

I quickly put my clothes back on not feeling myself and he notices.

"Rylee" he starts but I hold up my hand not wanting to hear everything.

"She missed your. She wants to be near you" I asked rhetorically already knowing the common signs of mate bonds.

He lets out a sigh looking tired which unintentionally hurts me.

"She was asking around for me. I didn't have my phone while we were looking for you and the Oliver mess. She came all the way to the pack territory this morning. I just went to talk to her and explain why I was away".

He takes a step towards me so I take a step back, knowing I can't handle touching him again.

"This can't go on forever, you know that right? The bond is there and it's getting stronger, even for a human"

"I know!" He growls out while throwing a side table into the wall. It didn't affect me. I was used to burst of anger and Alpha's lashing out for many other reasons. That was just a reminder of how different I was to her. She was gentle enough that she would have been breaking down at this point.

"I can't be here while you decide" I finally announce my worst nightmare. I was used to him fighting back and running after me. But one look at his eyes and I could tell he knew this was on him.

"I'll fix this" he says lowly.

"It's not something to fix Adrian. It's just fate" I whisper painfully while leaving his house. I hesitate outside stupidly hoping he might come after me.

After a slap in the face from my cruel fate, I call a friend to take me far away.

Chapter 17

I walked through the Silver Heart Pack crying my heart out to Scarlet for the first time. From Jax to Nathan to the worst loss of Adrian. I hold back on the gruesome details knowing her kind heart doesn't deserve that.

We cried together for awhile. I know she was conflicted with her anger for Nathan because I try to reassure her he doesn't deserve to be hated. His ongoing grief is punishment enough. That was also the moment I let go of any hate or fear I had towards him.

I've seen Julia and Nathan around the last couple days I've spent her and I saw why they worked together. I haven't talked to him yet but I know I was going to before I left again. This was another place it did not feel right to be in.

Once we get back to the house Zac wraps around Scarlet knowing he was feeling all her sadness. As she left to wash up Zac begin to tell me the same thing he has for the last two days.

"He called again. I told him you are doing fine, again"

I nod my head in appreciation now wanting to say another word about the matter. Every day he hasn't come back to me was another stab in my heart.

It just meant he was leaning closer to her. I couldn't blame him. I only blamed myself for believing it could work. For falling in love with someone that could never be mine.

The next day I felt brave. I took advantage of it and confronted Nathan during his trainings.

"Can we speak for a minute"

He just nods his head and follows me to the nearest park bench used for outside events.

"How are you doing? I-I uh was worried when you were taken"

"I'm going to be okay. I just wanted to say I'm happy for you and Julia" I barely choke out, feeling my fear and insecurities wanted to crawl out.

I could tell he was feeling uncomfortable as well. Knowing he rejected me and then shortly after chose someone else.

"It just works in a weird way. We both know what loss feels like and she understands I can never give her my entire self"

We say our goodbyes knowing we most likely won't cross paths again which seemed to be work best for both of us.

I decided to leave that night. I didn't tell Zac or Scarlet where I was going incase Adrian would call again.

After several hours I arrived at the familiar lake where I waited for someone to gather me into the territory. Alpha James welcomed me with open arms again.

He knew this wasn't my first choice but it felt like the most realistic choice. Far away from what I want and small enough for me to distract myself. I spent two weeks working under James, training with his small team, and avoiding my phone.

I wasn't happy but I was starting to think that it didn't matter anymore. James was a good friend whenever I let him in. One night we bond over strong whiskey and a venting session.

"The worst part is that I don't hate him. I still love him, always will" I drunkenly scream out.

"Hey at least you found love. Don't take that for granted"

"James why are you not searching for your mate. You need to get out there and look for her." I say a little too loudly.

His face turns serious for a moment thinking about what I just said.

"I've tried before and just decided to let it be up to fate. But maybe I should try again"

"Yes! Yes you should try again. Go visit the other packs. Go travel around. You deserve to find her"

After that night James called nearby packs to plan out his visits. He was gone for most of the days but the rest of his pack had his back including me.

After one week I heard rumors he was coming back with a few extra people. I knew that had to mean good news, that he found his mate. I joined the others around the lake waiting all wanting to see a glimpse of their Luna.

After many long moments I finally hear cheers and applause but I'm too far back in the crowd to see anything. I decide to just stay back and will eventually see them during their official mating ceremony.

I return back to my routine I have created here. I stop by the small orphanage and play with the few kids that live here. Eventually more people come by and talk about the new Luna, Ariel. I knew an Ariel from my original pack under Alpha Sam. She was Liam's little sister but she didn't train a lot and never traveled outside of the pack with us.

I decided to go to the pack house next to hear more of the gossip. Several people confirmed that it was the same Ariel I grew up around. I started to wonder if Liam joined her here which made me excited to see an old friend.

I walk with a little enthusiasm to James' house which I haven't felt in sometime. There was still a crowd around James when I got back but I did see Liam nearby, not surprised that he wanted to look after his sister even once she found her mate.

He spots me in the small crowd and runs up to me for a hug.

"I can't your sister is James' mate" I say while Liam let's go of me.

"Tell me about it. The age difference bothers me but he is a good guy"

We spend a few minutes catching up before he drops a bomb into the quiet life I just started for myself.

"I heard someone's been looking for you. An Alpha"

My eyes widen but I don't say a word. I can't.

"James seems to have protect you here since he's still looking. But he's even mad threats to Sam thinking he knows where you are. I think he's gone a little mad" he states with a little laugh at the end.

"Threats?" I whisper

"Ya it's been going on for over a week so not sure how long he will keep it up"

My mind wouldn't stop turning after that conversation. Why is he threatening other Alphas for my location? He knew where I was for days and didn't do anything about it.

I look back to see how happy James and Ariel looked. Adrian deserved to be that happy. I thought I let him go to be happy but I was willing to see him again if that would help him let go. I guess I was all about giving out closure

I went back to my room and turned on my phone. I unblocked his number and dialed it before I changed my mind.

"Rylee" he said almost in shock

"Adrian" I responded instantly

"Where are you Rylee. I need to see you. Please"

"Why are you searching for me?" I ask quietly, almost afraid

"Rylee I need to see you. I'll come to you. Please just tell me where you are"

"I'll come visit you" I finally said, knowing I would have an advantage going to him so I could plan an escape

"How soon can you get here?" It sounded like he said that with a smile.

"Probably tomorrow"

"I can pick you up" He tried to push again but I turned him down. I needed some control for this one. I didn't know what I was going to walk into.

The next day I asked Liam to help with travel plans. Thankfully he didn't mind traveling to Adrian's pack since he had some friends to catch up with. I always did like how easy going Liam was.

We spent house driving and goofing around just like we always have been. Of course he asked about Scarlet which he has always crushed on but I reassured him his mate will be just as lucky. I couldn't be the only one the moon goddess but a curse on.

We entered into the pack with familiar faces and drove straight to the pack house. I jump out giving Liam a hug knowing we would be going separate ways again.

As soon as we step back I heard a low grow behind me.

"Oh shit. I think he has lost his mind" Liam teases me and then walks away knowing there would be trouble

I turn around and see Adrian standing there as handsome as ever but with a murderous stance. I take a deep breathe and walk towards him, slowly letting his stare take me back to bliss.

Chapter 18

Adrian grabs my over his shoulders and storms off in the direction of his house.

"Adrian what the hell!" I scream out holding on tight. Adrian doesn't say a word until we're inside and be finally sets me down. He still looks furious.

"Tell me why the you came here with him?" He practically growls out

"He is an old friend and happen to be around to give me a ride" I explain, not wanting to anger the beast anymore. "It doesn't even matter. You tell me why you wanted to see me"

"Oh Rylee it does matter". Adrian comes close to me until I'm pushed up against a wall. He moves his hand to hold my face and comes inches close to my lips. "It matters because you're mine".

He lips capture mine in a slow sensual kiss. I kiss him back without thinking twice about it. I know my body would always crave him. He was the only man to touch me and I don't think I would want someone else to.

I moved my hands to the front of his shirt urging to remove any barrier between us. He quickly grabs my hands and puts them above my head.

"I love you Rylee" he breaths before kissing down my neck, sucking and nipping. I couldn't form any words. He continues to grind his body against mine until I let out a moan of frustration.

"Talk to me. Tell me what you want" Adrian whispers into my ear before continuing to lower his head to my breasts.

"Adrian" I moan out as he bits my nipple. "I want you inside of me"

Adrian gives me an wicked smile before moving down my body slowly removing my clothes. I find myself submerged in this moment, not wanting to risk anything to ruin it.

Adrian grabs my thighs and picks me up causing me to wrap around his waist. He carries me to his room while I run my own lips down his neck wanting to kiss every inch of his skin.

I yelp when I'm thrown onto the bed only to be covered by Adrian's naked body shortly after. His hands move down to my pussy growling when he sees how wet I am already.

I feel his erection against my entrance, already pushing himself in.

"Do you know why I'm always bare when I'm inside of you" he continues to move inside of me while I grab onto his shoulders in utter pleasure.

He knows I can't formulate any words as he continues talking, not missing a beat. "It's because you're mine. You've always been mind. No barrier. No obstacles"

He moves his hands to my ass to tilt me upward, feeling him even deeper than I've dreamed of. I moan out his name loudly knowing I was close.

As he lowers his head I faintly hear him growl "I'm going to mark you" before capturing my lips. That undid me. I dug my nails into his shoulders and moaned into his lips while my body releases itself.

A second later Adrian releases himself inside while leaving a few more lasting kisses on my lips and neck. I feel him playfully nipping that sensitive spot. I close my eyes enjoying his entrance.

My eyes snap open when I feel his sharp teeth teasing me even more. I push Adrian off of me not believing he would actually do it.

"What the hell Rylee", Adrian growing angry as I expected when I try to get away from him.

"You can't mark me" I mumble, the only string of words I've been able to say since he has touched me.

"Did you not listen to what I said. You're mine" Adrian growls before trying to get to me again. I quickly jump off the bed not giving him a chance.

"You let me leave, remember. Why did you let me leave" I hold back my tears trying to remain calm.

He curses under his breathe and tries to get to me again. I move out of the way again stealing one of his shirts to covering me up. I needed to focus on this and his touch was the ultimate distraction.

At this point both his hands have turned into first and there is a hole in one of his walls. Again this doesn't rattle me. I stay calm until he gathers himself to speak again.

"I rejected her okay. I told her the truth and we rejected each other. I'm free now. She understands to stay away. I'm free to be with you"

My mouth went slack. Everything I was hoping to hear was actually told to me. I let my tears fall down my face needed to feel something to believe this.

I let Adrian approach me this time, wiping away my tears, kissing my face.

"Rylee I'm going to mark you know. I can't wait any longer. I almost lost my mind when I couldn't find you"

He stares into my eyes so raw I had to look away. He runs his hands through my hair while bringing his head to my neck to continue his invasion. I climb my body onto his, holding tight, while he moves us back to the bed.

I scream out once I feel his teeth break my skin, leaving the lasting mark, making me his.

"I love you" I moan out once he releases his teeth and licks my swollen skin.

My eyes feel heavy as Adrian cuddles behind me.

"Go to sleep baby, I got you". I let the darkness take over, feeling whole again.

Chapter 19

The next month flew by. Adrian announced his new Luna to the pack which I was clearly nervous about. I had a feeling Adrian asked Grayson and Lexi to talk to the pack beforehand because I didn't hear any comments about us not being mates.

Of course I still had my doubts about Natalia, wondering what happened after I left. One night I managed to voice out my concerns while we laid together in bed.

"Will you still be seeing her? As friends?" I ask him while softly moving my fingers around his chest.

"No, we both agreed we shouldn't be in contact. "

I stayed quiet, not sure how to express all the other questions floating in my head. Adrian suddenly flips me and grabs my wrists to gain control over me. I was starting to see he would do that when he was nervous.

"Rylee please believe nothing happened between us. I had to explain our world to her and she understood it could not work. She has a family she wants to keep and she knows all we could ever had was a good friendship. I explained her the rejection process and we both agreed to do it to break the bond. This happened four days after you left. After that I spent every day looking for you"

I help my breath hearing every word coming from his mouth. He was breathing heavy now, still on top of me holding me tight. I lifted my mouth to capture his lips which he easily let me. I fought against his hands which made him let go of his wrists.

Before he changed his mind I quickly moved on top of him taking control. I rubbed my naked body against his, feeling him grow against me again that night. I easily moved down onto his erection, throwing my head back overwhelmed from the fullness.

I lean my hands back on his thighs and start to move rapidly against him. He doesn't touch me any further, just leaning back himself, watching me work out my climax.

As soon as I tighten against him and roll back my eyes, his hands jump back on my hips and flip me on my stomach. He enters me from behind without mercy and takes back his control.

After several hard thrusts, he lifts me up so I am on all fours and then continues to move smoothly against me. I moan out uncontrollably until he moves his hand to my neck and pulls me up so my back is against his chest.

I let me head fall against his shoulder, exposing my neck, silently begging for more. Adrian laughs against me, knowing he is torturing me.

Adrian slows down his movements and uses his other hand to softly rub my clit. It only takes a short time with a combination of his breathe against my neck, his hand pressure around my throat, and his other hand on my ideal spot.

During my climax Adrian throws my head back to the bed and drills into me, letting his own release out. I let out one more loan and fall against the mattress, completely destroyed in the most incredible way.

The next weeks we completed the mating ceremony, making me the official Luna of the pack. I was not intimated by this, being comfortable around Alphas and how packs are run.

What I found was that I intimated intimated by Grayson and Lexi. We would travel together to other packs and I noticed Grayson would always introduce her as his mate. I knew we could never have. It was petty and small but for some reason it still hit deep inside.

I expressed my concerns to Lexi one day, grateful we become close friends over these months. She told me I was being silly and she's sure Adrian has many plans for our relationships.

I thought her advice was vague but it did help me feel better so I shook it off and moved on.

———————————————————————————————

It's been a little over 8 months since our mating ceremony and I was starting to not feel well. Waking up nauseas and always tired. I knew I was expecting. It had to happen eventually since Adrian refused to have any barriers between us from the beginning. Even though I was extremely nervous to tell him.

We never actually talked about kids. He knew I spent most of my time at the orphanage to help take care of the kids but never talked about our own.

After a full morning of errands I went back to our room to take a nap, which was very unusual for me.

After what felt like five minutes I feel warmth from behind me that I snuggle into. I don't open my eyes until I feel a thick finger move up my thigh up to my entrance.

Adrian's breathe is hot against my face as I squirm against his finger needed more. After a lot of teasing he finally pushes himself on top of me gently placing his hands on my stomach.

I stop breathing for a moment knowing he's looking at me, wanting me to tel him, but I cant. He lowers his head to my breasts and slowly tortures me with his mouth, lightly bitting my nipples for my heightened pleasure.

This time my breasts are so sensitive I jump back from his bit. Adrian gives me a small smirk like he was expecting me to react differently.

I bit my lip, anxious to see what else he has planned. He continues to move his mouth lower to kiss every inch of my chest and stomach. I start to rub my thighs together to get some friction until he grabs them apart making a point that I'm under his control right now.

After worshipping my body, he moves back on top and lines himself to my entrance. Easily he moves in with how wet I already am. I moan out and let me head fall back onto the pillow.

Adrian grabs the back of my neck to move me forward to meet his eyes.

"Tell me" he whispers against my face while continuing to move inside of me. I can't string together any words while he continues to squeeze my neck looking unaffected.

"Rylee" he growls while moving his hands to my ass to life me higher against him. I grab his shoulders roughly and meet his thrusts.

I feel the liquid coming out of me in uncontrollably not caring about the mess I was making. I've never been this wet before which I know Adrian also notices by his loud moan, looking down at my body.

"Tell me Rylee" his voice changing to a soft tone while moving his hand against my stomach, but still moving against me.

"I'm pregnant" I whisper while holding his shoulders and eye contact. Adrian stops moving to look at my face, holding tightly to my hips.

After a moment of silence I see the reality set in on his face while he grins like a mad man. He pushes me back down on the bed while making the softest love to me. His mouth covers my lips, and then my neck, but mostly my breasts. I moan at the slightly touch, not used to extra sensitivity.

Adrian moves deeper, harder every time I react knowing it's a result from my body changes. He moves his hand to my clit knowing he's getting close. I lift my leg over his shoulder to give him better access.

We climax together, still continuing to rub against each other, not ready to let go of the heated passion just yet.

We lay together, forgetting that it's still daylight, forgetting that life is still going on around us.

"Are you nervous" I finally ask

Adrian moves his hand to my over sensitive breasts which have quickly become his favorite things to touch.

"Baby I've been ready for this since the beginning" he whispers into my ear while rubbing his hardness against me ready for the next round.

—————————The End —————————

www.ingramcontent.com/pod-product-compliance
Ingram Content Group UK Ltd.
Pitfield, Milton Keynes, MK11 3LW, UK
UKHW031950131224
452403UK00010B/705